"It's like making love."

King smiled. "We gotta move together, sweetheart."

At her unladylike response, King laughed aloud, then goosed the snowmobile up to full speed.

He felt good. The chase. The wind against his face. An adventure in the offing and no way to be sure of the outcome. That was what life was all about. That and a woman tucked up close against him. It had been a long time since he'd enjoyed such a potent combination.

In his imagination he had no trouble getting past her bulky clothes. He felt a heat that was at odds with the frigid temperature, and his thoughts progressed to the obvious conclusion.

Maggie in his arms. Pliable, hot and sweet.

ABOUT THE AUTHOR

As a child, Charlotte Maclay thought there were tiny
people inside the radio making up all those wonderful
stories. She tried to fool them by changing the stations
as fast as she could. Always, she failed. Then she grew
up and married an engineer who explained that those
voices were electronic—floating through the ether;
Charlotte's reply was "Sure." Years later she started to
use a computer and discovered the characters she'd
dreamed about had been hiding somewhere inside that
magic machine. She's delighted to be able to share some
of her fantasies with her readers. Charlotte and her
husband live in Southern California with their very
spoiled cat, Patches.

CHARLOTTE MACLAY

ELUSIVE TREASURE

Harlequin Books

TORONTO • NEW YORK • LONDON
AMSTERDAM • PARIS • SYDNEY • HAMBURG
STOCKHOLM • ATHENS • TOKYO • MILAN
MADRID • WARSAW • BUDAPEST • AUCKLAND

With thanks to Susan Naomi Horton for
graciously teaching me about PMF and PMI.
It works!

Published September 1993

ISBN 0-373-16503-X

ELUSIVE TREASURE

Chapter One

"What are you talking about, old man?"

"A treasure, son. Worth more than a million dollars."

"Gold?"

The wise old man nodded, his leathery face a map of weatherworn cracks and fissures. As he shifted his position, the Indian beads that were draped around his neck rattled together. "Yes, there is gold."

Leaning back in the deck chair, Kingsley McDermott stretched out his long legs and crossed his booted feet. The setting sun streaked the Pacific in silver ribbons that shimmered from the beach to the horizon beyond his Malibu house. His lips curled into a sympathetic smile.

"You need money, Whitecloud?" he asked the Indian, a man he'd first met years ago when they were both prospecting for the lost treasure of Durango. Or maybe it was in the Superstitions. After all this time, one treasure hunt tended to blend with the next. But their friendship had been a unique one, a relationship that had withstood both distance and time. At least, for King, the sense of connection had always remained.

"I'm too old to care about money," the Indian said. "But I'm telling you the truth about the gold. My people have known the tale for many years."

"Which of your people?" From his hard-angled features and wrinkled face, Whitecloud looked to be a combination of every tribe in the country.

"Those of the Shoshone villages, mostly."

King poured the man another tumbler of bourbon. He didn't know why Whitecloud had arrived unexpectedly at his front door, but he did that from time to time—and was always welcome. "Tell me the tale."

In a wary gesture, Whitecloud looked over his shoulder at the nearly deserted beach. Only a few hearty souls were out walking along the tide line, all of them bundled up in their jackets against a crisp spring breeze.

"It began a long time ago," Whitecloud responded, thoughtfully fingering the strand of beads hanging around his neck.

"Are you talking about one of your Great Spirit visions? Or is this for real?"

He widened his eyes in mild offense. "This tale is quite true, my friend. It started when the Union soldiers first came to California and began to drive my people out."

"The Shoshone weren't even in California."

He shrugged off the detail as having no consequence. "Our brothers the Miwoks, then. There was a great battle—"

"California Indians were peaceful."

"That is a lie, my friend. They rebelled under the yoke of—"

"The gold, Whitecloud. Get back to the gold." Tales of buried treasure had always amused King, but of late he'd felt restless and generally out of sorts, lacking his usual interest in pursuing lost causes.

"There was a small army outpost in Mariposa. My ancient brethren attacked them and the settlers, stealing many horses, which they drove up into Yosemite Valley. For food, I might add," he said with the dignity he'd gained while attending the University of California at Berkeley many years ago. "In one of the saddlebags was the army payroll, all in gold coins."

King straightened in his chair. This wild story had a certain ring of truth to it. But they all did, at first. Whitecloud was among the best weavers of tales. "Didn't the army go after the thieves?"

"Oh, yes." He looked over his shoulder again, then lowered his voice to a secretive whisper. "The Indians were massacred. Except for two young braves."

"The guys who had the gold, I assume."

"Naturally. They fled to the high country. Only years later did stories spread that they had hidden the gold in a cave north of what is now called Tuolumne Meadows in Yosemite. Do you know the place?"

"Not really."

"That whole area was a hunting grounds for my people. They summered in the high country and spent winters in the valley. Until the white men drove them out."

"You could say that about most of the United States."

Whitecloud shook his head, once again creating the distinctive sound of beads rattling. "You do not believe me, do you?"

"I need more than some Indian tale to send me off on a wild-goose chase." Though not much more, King conceded. The search, after all, was what he craved. He sure as hell didn't need any more money. In fact, he'd always had a dangerous amount of that particular commodity.

With another nervous swivel of his head Whitecloud reached into the pocket of his leather jacket. "I have a map. It will lead you to the greatest treasure of all. And I have this." He handed King a crumpled piece of paper and held up a coin for inspection.

A surge of adrenaline whipped through King's gut. Ignoring the paper for the moment, he carefully studied the ten-dollar gold piece, U.S. mint, dated 1860. "I'll be darned."

Smiling so his yellowed teeth showed, Whitecloud said, "Now you believe."

"I'm beginning to—"

There was almost no sound. Only an eerie whoosh, and then a red dot appeared in the center of Whitecloud's forehead, right above eyes that were wide open in disbelief—eyes that would never see again. Then the Indian slumped in his chair.

Shock immobilized King for an instant before his survival instincts cut in. In two steps he leaped over the deck railing and fell to the sand, coming up running for all he was worth. A natural-born coward, King wasn't about to wait around to see who was taking potshots at a guy with a treasure map. Particularly when the map was now in his hands. Whitecloud wouldn't have wanted him to take that kind of a risk.

Too bad he hadn't caught a glimpse of whoever had the gun. It might have helped the cops to nail him...or her. Poor Whitecloud. He deserved a better ending. King would miss his old friend. More than he cared to admit, he realized, as a great welling of emptiness filled his gut.

Damn! Real men didn't cry. Or so he'd been told. But that couldn't explain the sudden moisture in his eyes or the uncomfortable catch he felt in his throat. Whitecloud wouldn't want him to waste any energy on grief, either. Not now.

Ducking into an alley between houses, King stopped to catch his breath and steady himself. The way his heart was pounding, he knew he'd let himself get into lousy condition. His thirty-six years were evidently catching up with him. Maybe he should have accepted the neighbor's invitation to join her for morning jogs on the beach. She was a damn good-looking woman and her husband did a lot of traveling.

After making sure no one had followed him, King unfolded the faded map. The worn creases suggested it had been carried in somebody's wallet for a lot of years. But King knew that counterfeiters had ways to age paper that were pretty darn hard to detect. There were Indian markings—at least, what he thought were Indian symbols—written in the margins, and a whole lot of trails winding their way through what he figured was probably Yosemite National Park, based on what Whitecloud had said.

He smiled to himself and felt a familiar surge of excitement.

Another treasure to search for...and somebody else equally anxious to find it. By God, he wouldn't let Whitecloud's murderer get his hands on the gold. Of that he was damn sure.

Fortunately, he had a leg up on the competition. As it happened, he knew a woman who was probably the greatest expert on Sierra Indians in the country. Knew her rather intimately, as he recalled—in considerable detail, he mentally added.

Dear ol' Maggie Townsend.

God, thinking of her brought back a lot of memories. It also did something hot and insistent to his groin.

Somehow King doubted she would be all that pleased to see him.

For the moment, however, King figured he'd have some fancy explaining to do. Cops didn't always take kindly to treasure hunters mixing it up among themselves. Particularly when the results were fatal.

THE FRONT DOOR of the Sierra Indian Museum opened, letting in a gust of cool air, and the tinkling bell sounded its welcome to visitors. In response, Margaret Townsend lifted her head from her task of cataloging arrowheads.

At the sight of the man silhouetted at the door, her hands stilled and her breath lodged in her throat. Something about the breadth of his shoulders, and his narrow waist above long legs hugged into tight-fitting jeans, caused alarm bells to go off in her head. The old windbreaker looked so familiar. But it couldn't be...

"Hello, Maggie girl."

Her jaw brought her teeth together in a painful grimace. Nobody...*nobody* called her Maggie, much less Maggie girl. She was *Margaret*. Nice, quiet Margaret. *Studious* Margaret. With a Ph.D. in anthropology to show for her efforts. Only one man had ever had the nerve, the absolute gall to...

"King?" His name rasped up her throat in a harsh whisper.

"In the flesh, sweetheart." Even in the subdued light she could see his flash of white teeth.

She clasped the arrowhead in her hand so hard it cut into her palm. Her desire to shove the jagged point into King's heart, if he had one, warred with her basically pacifist nature. The pacifist barely won.

He sauntered toward her, his ridiculous snakeskin cowboy boots marking each long-legged step on the wooden floor and setting up a matching vibration right at the base of Margaret's spine. Her gaze was drawn to his thumbs hooked in his jeans pockets, his hands framing his slender hips. Like a thousand snapshots taken in slow motion, memories assailed her.

With the heat of anger creeping up her neck, she raised her eyes to meet his. "What are you doing here?" she asked, making no effort to conceal her lack of welcome.

"Is that any way to greet an old friend?"

She leveled a look into his silver-blue eyes that would have cowed a lesser man. "It takes two to make a friendship."

"You're not still mad at me, are you, Maggie?" He arched a questioning eyebrow.

"Mad?" Furious. Incensed. Outraged. Hurt beyond words. But not *mad*. That was far too simple a description of how she felt about King. "Of course not. Why should I be upset?"

"You never know about women. Some can hold a grudge." He picked up an arrowhead from the pile on the counter and shifted it in his palm. "How long has it been?"

Four years, eight months...and seventeen days. "I have no idea."

His gaze appraised her slowly, brushing first the top of her blond hair held back in a coiled French braid, then across her face in a lazy caress, and finally lowering to settle in almost a tactile caress on the rapid rise and fall of her breasts. "I've missed you." His voice was low and raspy and unfairly intimate.

She resisted the urge to step back from the counter...to *hide* under the counter. He was so damn cocky. "I sincerely doubt that."

"We had some good times together."

"You almost got me killed."

He shrugged. "How was I to know someone else had heard about a silver hoard in those Anasazi ruins in New Mexico?"

"There wasn't any silver. It was a hoax. And all I wanted to find were pottery shards. Just one little authentic shard would have made my day. And kept my employer at the Los Angeles museum happy." Coming back with only a broken heart to show for her efforts hadn't pleased anyone, most especially Margaret. Definitely unprofessional.

King replaced the arrowhead with the others. New Mexico had been quite a caper. As he recalled, it was the first time he had actually considered the possibility of chucking it all and settling down to a nine-to-five job with all the risks that entailed. Maggie had caused that dangerous aberration in his otherwise well-set course to maintain his freedom at all cost.

He'd gotten out of there just in time.

But not before he'd taught Maggie that there was something more to life than bits of clay.

Passion.

Once she'd caught on and loosened up that rigid veneer she wore like a chastity belt, Maggie had been the hottest number he'd ever known. Tight, moist and filled with a drugging nectar so sweet he could still recall her flavor. She'd managed to spoil it for him with anyone else.

Though King had been on the move a lot the past few years, he'd pulled out his memories of Maggie more than once—her hazel eyes bright with new discoveries, a shimmer of silver lashes fanning her cheeks, a sassy nose and sometimes a mouth to match.

She was remembering, too. He could see it in her eyes. Those angry sparks of gold tucked within the hazel circles glistened at him across the counter like flakes from King Tut's crown. With a slight curl of his lips King wondered what it would take to rekindle what they had had together. Not much, he suspected. If he played his cards right.

First, though, he'd have to deal with her temper. She was in no mood to forgive, much less... But then, how could he blame her?

"You haven't told me why you're here," Maggie said, her fists planted above the enticing swell of her hips. Her khaki skirt looked as if it had come off a rack of used army uniforms and her modest white blouse was buttoned tightly around the delicate column of her neck. She was still hiding, but she couldn't disguise herself from King. He knew the softness of her flesh and the caressable feminine landscape that lay just below the starched cotton fabric.

"Would you believe a social call?" he asked.

"Not likely."

He glanced around the room at life-size Indian models and an assortment of glass display cases filled with woven baskets, spears, wooden masks, plus other odds and ends of Indian artifacts. There was a general musty scent to the place that didn't quite camouflage Maggie's more inviting sultry perfume. "Nice museum," he conceded. "Small, but nice."

She lifted her chin. "We're very proud of our exhibits. The collection has grown considerably since I took over as curator last year. Our goal is to gain a national reputation... in a very specialized area, of course."

"Of course."

"I doubt the details of our plans would be of interest to you." Margaret finally unfolded her fingers enough to release the arrowhead that had been cutting into her hand. She examined the injury and brought her palm to her lips, licking the narrow line of blood.

"Hurt yourself?" The corners of King's eyes crinkled with amusement.

Before Margaret could stop him, King took her hand. A jolt of frantic sensory signals sped up her arm to scramble every rational thought in her brain. She watched in horror and fascination as he brought her palm to his lips, kissing her lightly. Sweet God in heaven! Why couldn't he have just stayed away?

"Don't," she protested in what was little more than a moan. She stared at his long, tapered fingers, their texture roughened and masculine compared to her fairer complexion. Strong, too, yet capable of incredible tenderness, and unfairly skilled in the art of making love.

"Dangerous business, this being a museum curator."

Feeling as though she'd been burned, Margaret snatched her hand back. "It wasn't till you showed up." In a futile effort she wiped her palm on her skirt. The heated feeling of King's lips wouldn't go away. Nor would the erratic rhythm of her heart slow down. "You were just about to tell me why you are here," she persisted.

"I've always been interested in Indians."

"Tell me another fairy tale." She nailed him with a look that brooked no further dodging of the question. "The only gold left in the Sierras has to be dug out one flake at time. We all know that's not your style."

"No need to be insulting."

No, indeed. What she'd rather do is yank out every curl of his silken brown hair one by one. Her fingers fairly itched to weave themselves through the tousled strands... and then draw his head closer to hers and feel his sensuous lips kissing her senseless.

She bit down hard on her inner cheek in the hope the taste of blood would block her thoughts. She would *not* remember his flavor, or his uniquely masculine scent, or how his hands had stroked her body to unbelievable heights of ecstasy.

"I think it's time for you to leave," she said, gathering herself and nodding toward the door.

"If that's what you want." He took a couple of steps away from the counter, just long enough for Margaret to let out a sigh of relief. Then he turned back. "I'm doing some research on local Indian lore. Perhaps you could refer me to an expert on the subject?"

"Indian lore?"

"Miwoks. Shoshone." He shrugged.

Margaret felt the blow right to her professional midsection. She prided herself on knowing more about California Indians and their native culture than anyone else in the business. "Just what was it you wanted to know?" she asked suspiciously.

"Nothing much." His confident smile told her she'd been had. He'd dangled the bait and she'd leaped right onto the hook.

"I'm listening."

"I've heard the Indians spent summers in the upper reaches of Yosemite and maybe lived in caves."

"They certainly hunted and gathered acorns and pine nuts all over the Sierras but there are only a few identified campsites." She thought a moment. In spite of the multitude of hikers in Yosemite during the summer seasons—herself included, when she had the chance—the area hadn't been well documented in terms of archaeological digs. It had been one of her dreams to discover some new site that would provide additional information about the primitive culture that had once thrived in the hills. "I don't recall any evidence of cave dwelling." Which didn't prove anything one way or the other. Maybe some day she'd have an opportunity to do a thorough survey of the high wilderness area.

He'd managed to edge back to the counter, close enough so she could see the little laugh lines at the corners of his eyes that the sun had failed to tan. His cheekbones were well-defined, his jaw strong and square. She'd always thought of him as exceptionally virile looking, not that she particularly valued a man's appearance, she sternly reminded herself. Handsome wasn't all that high on her priority list when it came to relationships. Commitment was far more important.

"If there were caves, there'd be pictures on the walls? Petroglyphs?" he asked.

A flutter of excitement stirred in her stomach. What did King know that she didn't? "Possibly. The Miwoks weren't noted as great artists."

"How 'bout the Shoshone?"

"More so. But why would you care about wall paintings?"

In a deviously casual gesture he raised his hand to her cheek. His fingers trailed slowly down to her jaw-line and across to her mouth in a suggestively smooth stroke. He rested one fingertip on her bottom lip. A shudder clear down to her toes rocked Margaret.

"Not every treasure a man searches for glitters with gold," he said in that soft, raspy voice. "How'd you like to join me on a little expedition?"

She bit him. Not all that hard, she conceded, but anything was better than standing there trembling, her eyes filling with tears for dreams that had never come true and her legs going weak in the knees. She wasn't about to make that mistake again. Not with King.

"I'm surprised at you, Maggie girl." In mock pain he shook his finger.

"Don't you call me—"

"I was only hoping the opportunity to make a new discovery would tempt—"

"Nothing you could say or do would tempt me, Kingsley McDermott." Not ever again.

"I have a map. I'm sure it's of Yosemite." He reached into his jacket pocket. "The problem is, I can't read all these Indian symbols, and I thought you'd—"

"You thought wrong." She marched from behind the counter to the front door and opened it. The bell tinkled merrily. She'd get rid of the damn thing the first chance she got.

"Good day, Mr. McDermott. As you're leaving be sure to put a contribution in the collection box."

"Maggie, if you'd just listen—"

"Out. Now." *And take the memories with you.*

Slowly he withdrew his wallet and dropped a few bills into the plastic container by the door. "You're making a mistake," he said.

"The mistake I made happened five years ago." She folded her arms across her chest. "I make it a point to learn from the lessons I'm taught."

For a moment she thought she saw a flash of regret in his eyes, perhaps even a spark of compassion. But before she could be sure, he was out the door. She supposed she'd just been imagining things.

She was already back behind the counter when she heard an engine start in the parking lot. A truck, by the sound of it.

He was leaving. *Good riddance,* she assured herself, ignoring the way her hand trembled and her vision blurred.

She rubbed at her eyes with the back of her hand. The lighting in here had always been dismal. Little wonder that she couldn't focus on her work.

It seemed as if only a few minutes had passed when she heard the door open again. It wouldn't be King returning, she told herself so she wouldn't be disappointed. He wasn't the kind of man who came back, much less apologized for a shattered heart or two along the way.

Plastering a brave smile on her face, she greeted the two museum visitors. Dressed in dark business suits, the men were about as opposite as you could get. The first was short, lean and absolutely bald. The other was a great hulking bear of a man with a bushy, dark beard to match. Odd couple.

"Good afternoon, gentlemen. Feel free to look around and if you have any questions, I'd be happy to try to answer them for you."

They didn't glance to either side. Instead they headed right for Margaret. She got a very uneasy feeling in the pit of her stomach.

"Ms. Townsend?" the shorter one asked.

"Yes. How can I help you?" She had a lot of funding requests out to various foundations, an effort to bolster a bare-bones budget for the museum. Maybe these men were here to check out the exhibits. She hoped so. If they were here to rob the place, they'd be disappointed. Except for the few bills in the collection plate, many more than usual since King had dropped by, she never kept any cash on hand. The way Hairy Bear walked past her and then came to her side of the counter was unnerving. The bulge in his jacket pocket was even more unsettling. "Was there something in particular you wanted to see?"

"I believe you are familiar with a Mr. McDermott?" Her head swiveled back when the short man spoke. These thugs could be dangerous. "And that he recently visited you."

God, what kind of a mess had King gotten her into now? "Yes, I know him, and he just left. I'm sure if you leave now, you can catch up with him." *Do let me hurry you on your way.*

"Did he show you the map?" the bald fellow inquired pleasantly enough. It was the other guy coming up behind Margaret that really had her nerves on edge.

"Look, I don't know what King is up to and I don't want to. He came in here, we talked and then he left. I don't know anything about a map."

"Ms. Townsend, we are in a bit of a hurry." He made eye contact with Hairy Bear over her shoulder.

The bulge in the guy's coat wasn't a gun. It was a knife. With a blade about four feet long, the tip of which now rested millimeters from Margaret's throat. Panic rose up in her like so much green bile. The next time she saw King she'd kill him and be done with it.

"Please. I don't know what King is after or where he was going. He can go to the moon, for all I care." For some inexplicable reason the word *Yosemite* wouldn't slip up her throat past the threatening knife.

"I believe you know more than you are saying, Ms. Townsend."

The knife pricked her skin. Hysteria threatened. How long did it take to bleed to death? she wondered frantically.

At the outer edges of her awareness she heard a sound in the storeroom. Dear God, one of her volunteers was due to arrive. She always parked in the back. If the sweet little lady was caught and killed by these madmen, Margaret would never forgive herself. A few petroglyphs weren't worth anyone's life, hers included. Though why on earth King was interested in primitive wall paintings was beyond her understanding.

"All right. I'll tell you anything you want to know."

The short man's narrow lips folded back over his teeth in what she took to be a smile. "A wise decision, Ms. Townsend."

Hairy Bear eased the pressure of the knife at her throat.

She swallowed hard.

An instant later a blurred figure in a windbreaker hurled himself through the storeroom door, bashed into hairy bear, knocking the giant to the floor, and leaped over the counter with an amazing amount of athletic grace.

"Don't even try it," King warned the short man.

"I believe you have something we want," he responded, circling to his left, his hand moving under his jacket.

King yanked a spear from the hands of a plaster Indian.

"Watch it, you guys," Margaret shouted. "I won't have any fighting in my museum."

The man at her feet groaned and struggled to his knees. She kicked at the knife on the floor beside him. It shot under the counter and banged against the wall.

When she looked up again Shorty had a large black gun in his hand pointed at King.

A cry of warning rose in her throat.

In a lightning-quick motion King used the stick end of a display spear to drive air out of short guy's lungs in a whoosh. Wood splintered. The gun skittered across the floor, crashing into a display case. Glass shattered.

Margaret screamed. "My exhibits!"

Grabbing her by the arm, King dragged her toward the door. "Come on, Maggie girl. We're gettin' outta here."

Chapter Two

"You're crazy!" Margaret cried out. "I'm not going anywhere with you."

King boosted her into the cab of his pickup, his hand branding her butt in an all-too-familiar way, and then he leaped into the truck after her. "Those guys are dangerous. Or didn't you notice?" He wrenched the key in the ignition.

"I was the one who had a knife at my throat, for heaven's sake. Of course I noticed." Her head snapped back with whiplash force as King accelerated out of the parking lot. The tires spun in the dirt and he nearly collided with a passing car on the highway.

She screamed, "You're doing it again, McDermott! You're going to get me killed."

"Not to worry, sweetheart. Everything's under control." He wheeled the vehicle into a tight right turn onto the main road and pressed the gas pedal to the floor.

The centrifugal force toppled Margaret against King. She struggled back to an upright position, ignored the momentary sensation of her breasts plas-

tered erotically against his muscular arm and snapped
her seat belt in place.

In any other town he would have been ticketed for
going so fast through a commercial zone, however
small it might be. But not in the tiny Sierra village of
Glenville. There was only one cop, and he was never
around when you needed him.

They whizzed by the post office and the small
shopping center that boasted a supermarket of sorts.
Then they were on a road lined by lodgepole pines that
flew by in a vague blur of green.

"King, will you please stop? You've got to tell me
what's going on."

"In a minute," he responded, glancing into the
rearview mirror. His shoulder still hurt from bashing
into the big man who'd had Maggie under his knife,
and adrenaline was still surging through King's blood.
He'd been scared nearly spitless when he'd circled
back to the museum and spotted the hulking car in the
lot. He'd recognized it immediately. Smooth-Head
Luke and his bodyguard, Little John, always traveled
first-class. They'd certainly had the biggest yacht on
the ocean during the Caribbean caper. Not that it had
mattered. Just as they had been retrieving the sunken
treasure, a hurricane had blown up, scattering Span-
ish doubloons all over the sea.

King chuckled to himself. Old Smooth-Head Luke
had turned so beet red he was lucky a blood vessel
hadn't burst. The man had a quick temper, that was a
given. But was he mean enough to kill Whitecloud?
King wasn't so sure.

"Would you like to share the joke with me?" Maggie's question had about as much warmth as an icicle. "I could certainly use a laugh about now."

"I was just thinking about the last time I saw those two guys," he admitted.

"You know those hoods?"

"Yeah. We're sort of in the same business."

"Harassing innocent women? Surely that can't be very lucrative."

He cast her a sidelong glance and felt his adrenaline rev up another notch. This time the cause was an entirely different kind of excitement. Definitely libido driven. "Depending on the woman, it can be quite satisfying."

Her back went stiff. Riveting her eyes on the windshield, she said, "I'd like you to stop and let me out. I can walk back to the museum. It's not that far."

"Not a good plan, sweetheart." He executed another turn, this time up what looked to be a private, circular driveway, and pulled the truck off to the side under a stand of trees. "Smooth-Head Luke and Little John are serious treasure hunters."

Her eyes widened. "Smooth-Head?" she asked incredulously. "That sounds like a comic-strip character."

"He's been bald since he was about twenty. I think he's probably sensitive on the subject, but that's what everyone calls him. Though not necessarily to his face."

"And he had his henchman prick me with a knife just because he wants a map for petroglyphs?" She rubbed at her throat. "That's very hard for me to believe, King."

"I may not have been entirely truthful with you, I admit, but there could be paintings in the cave. Indians did that sort of thing...when they got bored, I imagine."

Maggie placed her hand on the door handle. "From the beginning, King, or I'm out of here."

With no other choice, King told her about Whitecloud, omitting the painful detail of the Indian's death for fear it would truly frighten her. Like King, she was skeptical until she saw the coin.

"So you're telling me there's a whole hoard of these gold coins in some cave in the high country."

"That's the idea."

"How did your friend hear about this treasure?"

"Unfortunately, our, ah, discussion was interrupted before he gave me all of the details. I've known him a long time and I trust him, in spite of the fact he's sort of an Indian mystic. Great Spirit visions, that sort of thing. He gave me this map." King spread out the map between them on the seat. It looked like a photocopy of an original piece of parchment paper. "The problem is, these lines don't correspond to any trails on the park service maps. I figure they're Indian trails. You've hiked in the area. What do you think?"

"This is what your friends at the museum were looking for?"

"Yep. Don't know how they heard about—"

"Or how many copies have been made of this thing," she pointed out, a frown tightening her forehead.

In spite of her better judgment Margaret studied the map. She ought to simply get out of the truck. That would be the smart thing to do. But then . . . when had she ever been smart when it came to King? Sitting in the close confines of the truck, watching a little smile playing at the corners of his lips and seeing the glow of conviction in his eyes, Margaret found King a hard man to resist.

She also wasn't exactly thrilled about going back to the museum to face Smooth-Head Luke and company, all by herself.

"This is probably Tuolumne River," she said, indicating a wavy line on the map. "And clearly those markings represent mountain peaks, but there's not much way of telling..." She frowned. "There's an old diary at the museum. It was written by a trapper who lived with the Miwoks for a while and traveled with them over the mountains to trade with the Shoshone."

"I knew you'd be able to help me." His confident grin did something both warm and unwelcome to her midsection. "One little ol' cave in the mountains shouldn't be all that hard to find."

While she'd been examining the map his arm had slid along the back of the seat. Slowly Margaret became aware of his fingers fiddling with the fine hairs at her nape. His touch was so light and achingly familiar it was almost as though she imagined rather than actually experienced the sensation. A desire to relish the feeling warred with an uncharacteristically impulsive urge to break his fingers.

In the end she adjusted her position to remove both herself and King from further temptation.

"You're welcome to take a look at the diary," she said, her decision unwavering. "The museum is open to the public and anyone can make use of our archives. But that's absolutely all the help you'll get from me."

"Ah, Maggie girl, together we're such a great team."

"The answer is no." She folded the map with the same care she held her emotions in check. "Besides, in case it hasn't occurred to you, there may be signs of spring at this elevation, but it's still winter in the high country. That's not exactly a good time to go hiking—"

"That's why I got the snowmobile." He gestured over his shoulder to the truck bed, where a glistening blue machine was tied down with ropes, a detail Margaret had managed to miss when she'd been unceremoniously shoved into the vehicle. "No problem."

"No problem?" Margaret echoed. She could think of ten thousand possible difficulties a person could get into as winter slipped into spring in the high mountains. They started with blizzards and avalanches, then moved right along to exposure and frostbite. Not her cup of tea. But then, King had never been exactly conservative when it came to his life-style and taking risks. "Thanks anyway. I'll pass."

If truth be known, she doubted she would have accepted an invitation to walk in the park with King. He was far too dangerous a man for her to risk getting involved with him again. What she wanted was a nice, steady guy. Somebody who believed in putting down roots. A family man. For instance, she thought with a determined lift of her chin, a man like Robert Duran, a widowed schoolteacher with two children who were the apple of his eye. She'd been seeing quite a lot of him lately—*them,* she mentally corrected, recalling that the kids were always part of the package—and she'd be wise to continue that relationship, not renew an old one with King.

"Will you take me back to the museum?" she asked. "Or shall I walk?"

The silence of his indecision weighed heavily between them while a woodpecker beat staccato notes on a nearby tree and a slight breeze teased at the pine branches. King's gaze was steady on her, penetrating, touching her in a way she fought to resist. Once was enough, she reminded herself, even as she struggled not to smooth away the pleated furrow of his brow with her fingertips. He'd aged in the past few years, she decided. Around his expressive eyes she saw a weariness that hadn't been there four years ago. Maybe treasure hunting was hard on a man.

He still carried himself like an aristocratic pirate. All he needed was a black patch over one eye to complete the picture. The rugged angles and planes of his face, and a slender nose with a slight bend—the result of some long-ago fight, she imagined—were still the same. As were his lips. Full, sensuous and so mobile she always thought he was about to break into a smile. She remembered how—

A car passing on the highway broke the spell.

Pursing her trembling lips, Margaret decided that recalling how King's kisses had felt was a form of bittersweet punishment no woman should have to endure. She shouldn't have believed them then, and she shouldn't trust the same man now.

"Tell me, King, how did you manage to return to the museum just in time to save me from those thugs? Had you set me up?" she asked suspiciously.

"Me in cahoots with Smooth-Head Luke? Not a chance." He gave her an innocent look that didn't quite reach his eyes. But then, there was always a fair amount of devilment in those silver-blue depths. "I was coming back to ask you out to dinner."

"To wine and dine me so you'd get what you wanted?"

"Something like that," he admitted.

He'd probably had seduction on his mind, too, figuring she was still an easy mark. He couldn't know that with other men she was much more cautious in her relationships.

"So how about it?" he asked. "You name the place."

"Sorry. I have other plans for tonight." Like curling up alone with a good book. Safer by far than seeing any more of King. "Shall we go?"

With an easy shrug he turned away and started the truck, easing it smoothly back onto the road. Somehow, Margaret sensed he hadn't given up. More likely his devious mind was planning a new assault to gain her cooperation.

Under her breath she cursed herself for hoping he'd find some chink in her armor. She would simply have to brace herself for any eventuality.

KING CIRCLED THE MUSEUM twice before he parked in front. Besides Maggie's faded green Honda there was only one car in the back lot, an old Citroën. Hardly the vehicle of choice for Smooth-Head Luke.

Insisting Maggie stay behind him, King entered the museum first. What confronted him inside the building was twice as frightening as Little John and far more unpredictable.

"Easy does it, ma'am," he said to the woman, raising his hands above his head. Unless his eyes were deceiving him, she had an old Indian bow and arrow pointed at him. The contraption would probably snap apart if she let go of the arrow, but he wasn't willing to risk bodily harm. "I'm a friend of Maggie's."

"Margaret isn't here." The old woman's voice quavered in sync with her shaking hands, the arrow's aim jumping between his head and a far more important part of his anatomy. "I've called the police."

King could understand that. Most of the contents of every display case were strewn across the room. Broken glass was everywhere. Smooth-Head's temper had obviously gotten the better of him.

"It's all right, Estelle," Margaret said, stepping into the museum. "King's a friend—" Her voice caught as she surveyed the damage. A band of despair constricted her chest. So much wanton destruction. Irreplaceable woven baskets torn apart. Shattered wooden masks. The mere thought of trying to piece them together again was daunting. And how, given a minuscule budget and limited insurance, would she ever, *ever* replace all the display cases? Much less the priceless exhibits?

"Oh, Margaret, dear," Estelle cried, near hysteria, "I don't know what's happened. It must have been vandals. Terrible vandals. I came late and you weren't here and then I found..."

"Shh, Estelle, it's all right." Margaret gently took the weapon from the woman's hands and hugged her, as much for her own comfort as the woman's. "It's not your fault."

"But I should have been on time. I got to visiting with my grandchildren and the hour got away from me."

"The blame isn't yours. The safety of our museum is my responsibility." Margaret glanced over her shoulder at King with an accusing glare. "If anyone is at fault, I'm the one." *Guilty of having "friends" like King.*

"I'm sorry about all this, Maggie," King said, although his apology didn't do much good. "I don't even know how Smooth-Head Luke knew where to look for me."

"I think it would be best if you'd leave," Margaret insisted through tight lips. "As you can see, I have a great deal of work to do." She'd have to re-sort every darn arrowhead, find somebody who knew how to restore an olive-shell rope necklace and probably dry some new ones to replace those that had been smashed. The watertight baskets were a shambles....

She made a strangled sound that was somewhere between a laugh and a cry. "That's assuming the board of directors doesn't fire me on the spot." A totally reasonable reaction if they happened to learn of her former relationship with King.

"Hey, they wouldn't do—"

"Margaret dear, I'm going to get a broom." Estelle's hands fluttered about, generally indicating the storeroom. "Best we get started. At least clean up the glass before the police comes. He won't need to see... Oh, dear, what a terrible thing...." Her voice faded away as she shoved through the door to the back.

Estelle seemed a bit more under control now that she had something to do, which was more than Margaret could say for herself. She felt violated and used, her stomach knotted with righteous fury. Those thugs had destroyed her pride and joy. She'd lovingly arranged every display. Each artifact had a history, a personality that was as real to her as the man who stood studying the destruction with a detachment that riled her even more.

With the exception of her brief interlude with King, Margaret had always made her decisions based on her professional goals. The Sierra Indian Museum was important. If not to anyone else, it certainly was to Margaret. She was going to make it into the best darn little museum in the country. Whatever it took.

By God, she wasn't going to let King and his treasure-hunting cronies get away with this. They all believed there was gold stashed somewhere in the mountains. She'd fix them. She wouldn't just get mad. She'd get even.

"The gold coins you mentioned. Just how much money are we talking about?" she asked. She casually fingered a quill headband that fell apart in her hands. With a determined lift of her chin, she renewed her resolve.

King raised a curious eyebrow. "Whitecloud said there was a million dollars' worth of coins."

A fortune. More than enough to repair the damage to the museum and still expand the exhibits. "Very well. I'll take half."

"Say that again?"

Daring him to argue with her, Margaret squared her jaw. "I'm going with you, King. We're going to find that damn treasure and half of it will belong to the museum." She marched across the room to stand nose to chin with him. "Have you got that straight?"

"Yes, ma'am." A smile started at the corners of his mouth, then swept up his face until his silver-blue eyes sparkled with both mischief and triumph.

Within Margaret's traitorous body she felt a response, the forbidden thrill of excitement she'd only experienced with King. In that moment she knew she'd probably made the worst mistake of her life. But now there was no turning back. The future of the museum, and her career, were at stake.

MARGARET TUGGED ON the oversize snowmobiling gloves that matched the designer thermal-layered suit King had provided. "You certainly were confident I'd want to come along on this trip." He'd had the supplies in the back of the truck the whole time, including this aquamarine-colored outfit for her.

As he pulled on his shiny black jacket, he winked.
"I figure I'm pretty irresistible when I set my mind to
it."

She was hardly in a position to argue the point, but
she wasn't about to admit it aloud. "But how did you
know my size? It's been years since we..." *Were lovers,* but she didn't dare say that. "Since you last saw
me."

He gave her a slow, appraising look filled with
masculine approval. "Some things a guy simply
doesn't forget."

That went for a woman, too, she realized. Margaret could have walked into any men's department
and picked out a shirt just right for his broad shoulders and tapered waist...and done it blindfolded. The
tactile memory of his breadth and shape was that
strong. Pleasure rippled through her body at the realization that his recollections were equally accurate.

Suppressing a sigh, she turned to absorb the scenery. She and King, along with Estelle, had hastily
cleaned up the worst of the museum carnage. Then
they'd made their brief report to the police and Margaret had locked up. She would be gone only a few
days, she'd assured her faithful volunteer. Then she'd
be back with money to start anew.

King had driven so quickly through Yosemite Valley that there'd been little time to gain more than an
impression of crowded roads, majestic granite cliffs
and the sound of roaring water tumbling over falls that
had just come alive with early spring melt after a long
winter.

To her dismay King had simply ignored Road Closed signs on Tioga Pass, the highway that led to the high country. He'd actually picked the lock on the barrier. Rather professionally, she thought. No doubt he had other skills of dubious merit she hadn't yet noticed.

Now they stood near the seven-thousand-foot marker on a winding road to Tuolumne Meadows, knee-deep in snow that was too much for his four-wheel-drive vehicle to manage. In the slanting rays of afternoon sun the stunted pines looked black and foreboding. Margaret shivered in the oppressive silence. Winter still had a firm grip on the land at this altitude.

She zipped up her jacket. "Are you going to leave your truck here?" He'd parked it off to the side of the road in a snowdrift that came up to its windows.

"Sure. We'll pick it up on the way back. Or when the road's open this summer. No hurry."

He certainly seemed unconcerned with what appeared to be a brand-new and very expensive vehicle. The dealer's sticker was still attached to the side window. Money had never been important to King. She wondered again, as she had years ago, why he bothered searching for treasure.

"Here you go, sweetheart," King said. "Your backpack."

He eased the straps over her shoulders and cinched the belt around her waist. The weight pressed her deeper into the snow. "Where's yours?" she asked, glancing around.

"My gear's stowed in the saddlebags on the snow-mobile."

"Do you really think that's fair?"

"We're going to ride double. There wouldn't be room for you if I had a pack on my back."

His logic was unassailable, and irritating as hell. "Let's get on with it, then." She brought the visor of her helmet down with a resounding snap.

"Time to check out the communicators," he said. "Can you hear me okay?"

The transmitter-receiver built into the helmet had all of the hi-fi quality of an empty tin cup. "I hear you fine."

He gave her one of those grins that stirred up the butterflies in her stomach, then tugged on his own helmet. The glistening black plastic gave him a dangerous look, and that was what he was...*dangerous* to a woman's peace of mind.

At King's urging, Margaret straddled the snowmo-bile. He settled in front of her. Actually, that wasn't an accurate description of what happened. He placed his butt right up against the apex of her thighs, thighs that were now pressed along the length of his much more muscular legs. In spite of the bulk of winter clothing, she was acutely aware of how she was strad-dling not only the machine, but King, as well. There was nowhere to hold on except around his waist. In-viting territory, she admitted, but not when she was experiencing such vivid reminders of what they had once been together.

Once under way, her problems were compounded. The vibration of the machine, and how King's body moved against hers, sent erotic signals to her nether regions that she didn't want to acknowledge. With little other choice, she plastered her head against his broad back and held on tight, catching his musky, masculine scent the new clothing didn't quite disguise.

Fortunately, the ride couldn't last forever.

King squeezed the accelerator. Getting used to the feel of the machine, he made a series of tight S-turns that took them from one side of the road to the other.

"Hey, what are you doing?" Maggie complained over the hum of the engine. "You're going to dump me off."

"Just stick with me, Maggie girl." As she tightened her grip around his middle, King smiled. "It's like making love, sweetheart. We gotta move together."

At her unladylike response King laughed aloud, then goosed the snowmobile up to full speed.

He felt good. The chase. The wind pressing against his visored face, an adventure in the offing and no way to be sure of the outcome. That was what life was all about. That and a woman tucked up close against him. It had been a long time since he'd enjoyed such a potent combination.

Most women wouldn't look very sexy in bulky winter clothing and a helmet. Maggie did. In his imagination he had no trouble at all getting past a few zippers and snaps. Heat that was at odds with the frigid air temperature stirred in his groin and his thoughts progressed rapidly step-by-step to the obvious conclusion. Maggie in his arms. Pliable, hot and sweet.

His need to feel more than her breasts against his back and her legs squeezing his thighs was a physical pain that had only one antidote. He wanted to surround her, fill her. The tightening of his muscles reminded him just how good it could be.

Not that she was equally eager, he reminded himself with a twinge of regret. Indeed, the fact that she was reluctant made her downright *dangerous*. King had never been able to resist a challenge. Uptight Margaret Townsend was the kind of lady who liked strings attached. She'd almost hog-tied him once, whether she knew it or not.

Over the next few days King would have to remember that. For her sake as much as his, he realized with considerable regret.

As they arrowed along the mountain highway the stunted pine forest gave way to an alpine meadow dotted with snow-covered boulders, like a huge plate of lumpy marshmallow sauce. On the horizon the last rays of sunlight cast the mountain peaks in a strawberry glow.

King slowed the snowmobile.

"There's a skiers' shelter at the Tuolumne Ranger Station," he said, the built-in communicator picking up his voice and transmitting it to Maggie. "We'll spend the night there."

"The rangers aren't going to be pleased we've come by snowmobile. They're likely to arrest us and throw away the key. I'm sure we're breaking a dozen different laws."

"I'll give 'em my innocent, blue-eyed look. Works every time."

It probably did, Margaret conceded. At this point she didn't much care. She felt permanently frozen to both the machine and King's back. In spite of her heavy clothing the cold had seeped through every crack and cranny to turn her blood into so many icicles. Her muscles ached. What she needed was a good night's sleep in a soft bed in some place very warm. The Hilton in Palm Springs sounded about right.

A few hundred yards from the highway a stone cabin nestled among the pines. Above it, patches of corrugated tin roof blown clear of snow glistened in the fading light, and smoke drifted lazily from a chimney.

Pulling up in front of the cabin, King cut the engine. He unsnapped and removed his helmet.

Silence, so heavy it weighed on his inner ear with a sound of its own, washed over him.

"Off you go, Maggie girl."

She groaned. "I'm not sure I can move."

With a certain amount of reluctance he unfolded her arms that had been wrapped securely around his waist. "A few deep knee bends will fix you right up."

"Don't even think about it. I'd break for sure."

Laughing, he helped her off the machine. She stomped her feet in the hard-packed snow to restore circulation, and he did the same. When she removed her helmet, her long blond hair came loose. She shifted it gracefully from side to side across her shoulders and King felt that hot curl of wanting slide through him again. This was how he liked her. Her hair...and spirit...free. Just as she'd been for him in New Mexico.

It was all he could do not to drag her hard up against his body and kiss her until she remembered every kiss they'd ever shared. The pleasurable thought ricocheted around in his brain until he recalled the need to go slowly.

"So how do you like the trip so far?" he asked, quirking his lips.

"I don't think I'm built right for riding that monster."

He gave her a slow, appraising look that ignored her clothing and went right to the subject he had in mind. "That's okay," he said, his voice husky. "You're built just right for the things that matter."

Something sparkled in her eyes... anger or excitement. The stigmata of cold on her cheeks gave her a flushed look that could have been taken for sexual desire. She was telling him things he wanted to hear. Interest. Readiness. Willingness to be persuaded. King doubted she knew how well he could read her. But then, he'd had a fair amount of experience. Much more than Maggie had.

Maybe she didn't know what she did to him, he considered. She was usually so prim and proper other guys might not be able to see her potential—all that passion so close to the surface. Maybe no one had shown her. It might be only male arrogance, but he liked to think he was the only guy who knew what a hot little number Maggie could be. Truth was, he couldn't handle the thought that she'd shared so much with anyone else.

"King, whenever you're through...doing whatever it is you're doing, I'd like to get in out of the cold." Though she was clearly trying for brusque, her words came out more like a breathy whisper and the flush on her cheeks had deepened.

King chalked up one more for hidden messages he liked to hear. "Good idea," he conceded. The temperature was dropping fast along with the setting sun.

He turned toward the cabin just as a figure rounded the corner coming in their direction.

The olive-drab uniform and parka looked like standard issue for a park ranger. The wearer, however, was far from King's image of your typical Smoky the Bear or Ranger Rick.

A knockout, she sauntered across the snow as if it were a stage at a Vegas nightclub. The way she shifted her hips oozed sex appeal. Her dark hair, almond-shaped eyes and oval face combined in a studied, sultry way that was anything but innocent. She sizzled. And knew it.

"Well, hello there," King drawled. "Nice neighborhood you've got here."

Chapter Three

For thirty minutes Margaret stood in the snow fuming.

King was actually flirting with the park ranger. His gaze teased over the woman in an appreciative way that made Margaret want to gag, and his lopsided grin was producing about a million megawatts of sex appeal. God, he'd used the same charm on her, she realized, and she'd fallen for it—hook, line and broken heart.

In return, the ranger's long lashes batted her cheeks like a pair of black moths captured and glued in place.

Ever since they'd arrived, King and the woman had chatted amiably while Margaret's toes were turning to ice cubes.

"Excuse me," Margaret interrupted in a tone she hoped would cut through their instant intimacy. "I understand there's a skiers' shelter?" Someplace warm where she could reconsider this whole expedition.

The woman, who had introduced herself as Diane, let her eyes flick over Margaret in a dismissive gesture and quickly returned her full attention to King.

"You really must come to the party this evening," the ranger said in a honeyed voice. "My cabin. Eight o'clock. It's a rather spur-of-the-moment thing. Just a little fun to break up the boredom. Bring your friend, too, of course."

Margaret could almost hear the unspoken *if you must.*

"We'd be delighted," King agreed. "I'm only sorry I didn't think to bring something to enhance the celebration."

Margaret rolled her eyes. It was obvious that this little tête-à-tête would go on for a while. She'd have to find her own way to the shelter.

Hefting her pack over one shoulder, she glanced around. From the look of the footprints in the snow, a path led off to the right of the ranger's cabin. As she started in that direction a beautiful German shepherd appeared at the corner of the building. He sat down and cocked his head. A low growl rumbled in his chest.

"Hi, fella," she said. "Aren't you a pretty boy." Turning back to the ranger, she asked, "Your dog?"

Diane's gaze darted from Margaret to the dog and back again. "Ah, yes, that's George. Here, Georgie," she called sweetly. "Be a good boy and come to Mama."

The dog didn't budge. Not even a twitch of his tail. Odd.

"Have you and your dog been up here alone all winter?" Margaret asked.

"We get lots of visitors. They're all very friendly."

I'll just bet, Margaret thought with a fair amount of ill will. She pictured an unending line of male cross-country skiers winding their way up from the valley floor with a lot more than exercise on their minds. King, no doubt, would be in the lead. Not that it was any of her concern.

With a determined shrug she turned away again. She'd taken only a few steps when, to her surprise, King fell in beside her, lifting the pack from her shoulders.

"Here, let me carry that for you."

"A true gentleman," she responded without a corresponding smile of thanks.

He frowned. "Is something wrong, Maggie?"

Gritting her teeth, she said, "Of course not. Why would you think that? After all, what woman wouldn't enjoy standing out in the cold, freezing her buns off and being totally ignored, while you try to hit on the local ranger?"

"Why, Maggie girl, do I detect a note of jealousy?"

"Certainly not." She'd never admit that to either King or herself, though she suspected there might be a nub of truth to the accusation—a possibility she was determined to ignore. "Your relationship with other women is entirely your own business."

"Hey, she's as phony as hell. I know that. I was only using my baby-blues to get on her good side. No sense to have the ranger upset with us before we even get started looking for the gold."

Margaret halted midstride. At least he'd recognized the femme fatale for what she was. "Did it oc-

cur to you that your charms weren't necessary? That
woman didn't say word one about us arriving by
snowmobile. And I'm sure motorized vehicles aren't
allowed up here this time of year. After all, the road's
closed." To anyone who wasn't skilled at picking a
lock. "Most park rangers would have been livid that
we were violating all of their rules."

"Maybe you underestimate my charm."

Not likely. Margaret had fallen under his spell so
quickly the first time they met she wasn't about to
discount King's seductive skills at this late date.
"Come to think of it, she didn't even ask if we had a
backcountry permit when you told her we'd be doing
a little exploring. In the summer I always have to fill
out forms about where I'm going and how long I'm
going to stay. I have to list every campsite."

"Don't worry about it, Maggie. We'll be gone tomorrow. No sweat."

Margaret didn't share his confidence. She had the
distinct impression something wasn't quite right. Beyond the fact that any park ranger worth his or her salt
should have been upset, Diane seemed far too interested in finding out about their plans. Fortunately,
King had been a bit vague on the details.

Arriving at the skiers' shelter interrupted Margaret's suspicious thoughts. She'd so rarely felt any
emotion that resembled jealousy, perhaps she was
leaping to unwarranted conclusions, she decided, too
weary to give the problem more thought.

To say the shelter was rustic overstated the case.

Four sets of iron bunk beds, with mattresses mea-
suring no more than an inch thick, lined two of the

rock walls. A scarred picnic table boasting a sooty kerosene lantern filled the middle of the room. Fortunately, a fire blazed a welcome at the far end of the cabin, filling the room with the delicious scent of wood smoke. It wasn't the Palm Springs Hilton, but it was warm and would have to do.

Shivering, Margaret headed toward the fire, giving the other occupants of the shelter a quick smile. They were an eclectic group of wiry athletes with long, stringy hair, plus one guy who looked as if he could be a linebacker for the Rams. No doubt she'd get to know them all later. For now her priority was simply to get warm.

King hefted the saddlebags from the snowmobile onto an upper bunk. As he eyed the people sitting around the table, he got an uneasy feeling. He didn't like the predatory way the big one was looking at Maggie.

"Hello, little lady," the guy in question said in a suggestive drawl. "I'm Arnold Czonka. Welcome to our humble abode."

King wasn't pleased with Maggie's quick smile as she introduced herself. He purposefully walked across the room and stood between her and the oversize lummox at the table. "I'm McDermott and she's with me."

Arnold stood. All six foot four and three hundred pounds of him.

King wondered if he'd made a tactical error.

"The lady's with whoever she wants to be with, buddy," Arnold said.

Holding the guy's gaze, King said, "Why don't you and your friends stick to your own business. It'd be a lot healthier that way."

"For me, or for you?" Arnold challenged.

"I hope you've got your medical insurance all up-to-date," King returned.

Margaret pulled off her gloves, not pleased with the animosity in the room. Or was it jealousy on King's part? she wondered, but quickly discarded the idea. More likely he was afraid she'd be distracted from helping him find the treasure.

On the other hand, this was no time for King to start a fight. She didn't much care for Arnold's wild-eyed look—as if King were a quarterback he was itching to sack.

"I hope you gentlemen are planning to go to the ranger's party this evening," she said, trying to break the tension. "I'm sure it will be a lot of fun."

For several long counts King and Arnold stared at each other. Margaret felt as if they were posturing, rather like bull moose in mating season. Men didn't usually do that around her. It gave her an odd sense of power.

BY EIGHT O'CLOCK that evening Margaret decided her fellow occupants of the skiers' shelter were definitely not party animals. It appeared even Arnold had decided to back off after King's warning. In fact, the men appeared to be very much engrossed in themselves.

The contingent from the shelter had moved their war stories about assorted skiing adventures from one location to another, taking up their new positions around the fire in the ranger's cabin.

Margaret was listening to their tales with little interest when King slipped up behind her.

"Let's get out of here," he suggested, his hand possessively at the small of her back.

She raised her eyebrows.

"If I hear one more time about how that skinny guy almost made the Olympics, I'm going to stop sending my annual contribution to the U.S. team."

In spite of herself, Margaret laughed. "He is a little full of himself, isn't he?" she whispered. Even Arnold, who had done his share of verbal strutting, looked bored with the young man's bragging.

She picked up her jacket from the back of an old overstuffed couch and King did the same with his, tugging it on over his wool sweater without closing the zippered coat. As they quietly slipped out of the cabin, Margaret realized the ranger had done a vanishing act, too. *Some hostess,* she thought.

The cold outside air tingled Margaret's cheeks and her breath fogged in front of her face. A full moon cast bright shadows across the ground, turning the snow into silver paths that wound through the trees and off across the meadow. King chose a direction that led away from both the cabin and the shelter.

In the stillness, only their boots creaking in a matching rhythm on the snow broke the silence. No wind shifted the darkened tree branches. No animals stirred in the night. Just Margaret and King, together in the intimacy of a vast land.

She was acutely aware of his nearness, the length of his stride and his strong profile shadowed by a moon almost as bright as day. Just in the way he carried himself King radiated power . . . and male sexuality. A seductive combination difficult to resist.

She swallowed hard. Maybe taking a walk with King was not a good plan. She was having a hard time avoiding thoughts of deep, penetrating kisses, warming caresses and hot, sweaty bodies. Hers and King's. Together. Memories that would be better off left in the deep freeze of the past.

"Did you know the Inuit have a dozen different words for snow?" he asked, once they were well away from the cabins.

Relieved that King had chosen a neutral topic that would get her mind off other, forbidden subjects, she replied, "I guess that tidbit of information has escaped me. Arctic natives aren't my specialty."

He scooped up a handful of snow. "I was up near Nome a few years back. Interesting country. Winters are the very devil, though."

She wondered if there was any area of the world he hadn't visited in search of his elusive treasures. A woman would be foolish to try to slow his rolling stone. That's what Margaret's mother had done. Tied herself to a dreamer, a man who kept trying to invent the equivalent of a better mousetrap, failing in the effort more times than not. And mentally abandoning his wife and daughter in the process.

"I think I've decided what kind of snow this is," King continued.

"What kind is that?" Belatedly catching a mischievous gleam in his eye, she knew the answer. With a groan she retreated a couple of steps. "Now, King..."

He followed her. "Perfect for snowballs."

"No. Wait a minute. You have to give fair warning," she protested, excitement and laughter bouncing against her heart. He'd always had an uncanny ability to make her laugh, even when she didn't want to.

"All's fair in love and snowballs."

"But your hands are bigger than mine." She whirled away. Slipping and sliding, she dashed off the path into the pines. She circled one, putting it between her and King, and tried to scoop up a snowball in self-defense. Too late.

He lunged toward her.

She feinted right, then ran to the left, laughing and breathless, aware that for all his craziness King was more fun to be with than any other man she'd ever known.

King was too quick for her. Like a scene out of a B movie they collided, and suddenly they were a jumble of arms and legs, collapsing in laughter on the ground. His weight pressed down on her.

For a moment Margaret was excruciatingly aware of how their entwined position mimicked a far more intimate act—one she remembered in exquisite detail and didn't dare think about.

The second he made the same connection, she knew. His muscles went taut and he drew a sharp breath. Laughter no longer rang in the air, which had now grown sultry with the heat of desire.

Warning alarms sounded within her brain.

Reacting instinctively, as though her survival depended upon escape, she scrambled away. Even as she struggled to her feet she was conscious of where their bodies had met—places on her arms and thighs and across her breasts that now carried the heated residual of the all-too-brief contact.

He was a little slower to get up. For an instant she had the advantage. Using two hands, she scooped up some snow and rained it down on him. Flakes caught on his brown hair, glistening in the moonlight.

"Ah, a fighter," he said with a treacherous laugh. "I'll get you for that, Maggie girl."

"You started it." She ducked a well-thrown snowball that grazed her hip, then turned and ran in the opposite direction. The deep snow dragged at her feet.

A moment later King was on her heels. She felt snow spray across her back in an icy caress. A part of her wanted to turn, to throw herself into his arms and feel his mouth warming her lips as only King could. But a wise woman wouldn't risk that, she reminded herself.

Something caught her ankle—a root or downed branch, perhaps—and she found herself tumbling head over heels into the snow, landing on her back with a soft puff. She blinked and looked up at the stars. Then King's face blocked her view.

"Are you okay?" He knelt beside her, his voice concerned, his cold hand gently palming her overheated cheek.

Margaret's heart hammered against her ribs. In that instant they were frozen in a silent tableau, their breath clouds mingling in the few scant inches that separated them. She inhaled deeply of his spicy scent, knowing that she hadn't been all right since the day he'd left without saying goodbye. But she wouldn't tell him that.

She levered herself into a sitting position. "I'm fine." Her words came out in a breathless whisper. If she just leaned forward again, he'd kiss her. She was sure of that. It was in his eyes and the way his gaze focused intently on her lips. She felt her stomach muscles go tight in sweet anticipation.

His fingers shifted to the tips of her hair and he toyed with the strands momentarily. Somewhere deep inside her body Margaret sensed a spreading heat, like a spring thaw coming to the mountains.

Lord, she didn't dare let that happen. Not with a man who thought looking for lost treasures was how to spend his life.

"King, has it occurred to you that you've never quite grown up?"

His rakish grin had a boyish quality that tugged at her heart, in spite of the fact she should have known better. She turned her head to avoid his touch . . . and the urgent feelings he created.

"I hope I never do," he agreed easily, sitting back on his haunches. "Life is too short."

"But why? You're capable of so much."

"Maybe I simply never had a chance to be a kid when I was young. That happens when you grow up lockstepped with a bodyguard."

"You had a bodyguard as a child?" Astonishment raised the pitch of her voice.

"Yeah. And let me tell you, a fella really gets razzed in the boys' locker room about having a baby-sitter. It made it pretty darn awkward to go out for sports." He stood and offered his hand to help her to her feet.

Ignoring his obvious strength and the ease with which he helped her to a standing position, she said, "But why did you need—"

"Let's just say my folks were a bit overprotective." He shrugged as she quickly removed her hand from his grasp. "Once I got out of the house, I swore I'd always take care of myself."

Without any encumbrances, she suspected—like a wife. What a strange childhood he must have had.

Sighing in frustration, Margaret brushed the snow from the back of her pants. "It's getting late. If we're going to be up and going in the morning, we'd better get some sleep."

"Let's hope the ski crowd has settled down for the night."

King could have hoped for a lot of other things— like a private cabin with a nice, big bed to share with Maggie. Bunks and roommates who were likely to snore were a poor, if fortuitous, substitute. At least the situation would keep him from getting carried away with the moment.

Truth was, he'd almost lost it with Maggie a minute ago. A reckless urge that would have led to nothing but trouble. For them both. Her unique combination of innocence and underlying passion did a real number on his libido.

He was going to have to watch himself.

Shoving open the door to the darkened shelter, King let Maggie precede him inside.

He'd just stepped over the threshold when he felt his feet violently lifted a foot off the floor. His body slammed hard into the rock wall, knocking the air out of his lungs.

Maggie screamed.

"What the hell—" King choked. Some guy with big, meaty hands had him by the throat.

A match flared.

King smelled Arnold's sour breath on his face. His mouth went dry and he told himself it wasn't from fear. He could take this guy, given a chance. Size wasn't everything.

"All right, hotshot," Arnold said in a voice deep enough to be a growl. "You've been asking for trouble ever since you showed up. We want our money back or it'll be your neck."

One of the skinny kids got the kerosene lantern going again. It gave off more smoke than light.

Maggie tugged fruitlessly on the behemoth's arm. "Leave King alone," she cried.

"I don't know what you're talking about." King forced the words past the narrowing of his windpipe, suppressing a wave of panic. If he just stayed cool, he and Maggie would be all right. "I haven't got your money."

"No? Well, we're all missing stuff outta our packs. You and your sweet lady friend left the party early. We all saw you go. So we figure..." The big hand squeezed more tightly around King's neck, cutting off his air. "You two had to be the ones who took our stuff."

"You're wrong," Maggie protested, trying to wrap her arm around Arnold's neck to pull him off. A courageous gesture but futile, King considered, his vision blurring. The guy was built like a Sherman tank. Sheer force wouldn't overpower him—not that Maggie had enough strength to even come close.

"We've been out walking," she persisted. "That's all."

Arnold made the mistake of trying to shrug Maggie off his back, easing his grip on King's throat in the process.

King took advantage of the lapse.

With as much force as he could muster King raised his locked fists, breaking Arnold's hold on his neck. At the same time he lifted his knee into his opponent's groin, then drove his elbow into the guy's gut. This was not the time to fight fair. Old Whitecloud had taught him that. He could almost hear the Indian urging him on.

A moment later King had a cursing Arnold face-down on the picnic table, his arm bent behind his back at a very uncomfortable angle. Breathing hard, King leveled the other skiers a warning look. "Stand easy, gentlemen. I don't want to have to hurt anyone." *Or be hurt,* he mentally added. A sore throat was enough damage for one night. Violence was not his style.

"Now you..." King nodded at the wanna-be Olympian. "Tell me what the hell is going on."

The kid cowered back a step or two. "When w-we came back to the shelter, well, the place was a mess. All our gear...money..."

King scanned the room. Odds and ends of camping paraphernalia were strewn on every bunk along with a couple of open wallets. He cursed under his breath. It was entirely possible Whitecloud had blabbed about the treasure to a lot of folks, all of whom were now looking to get a piece of the action.

He glanced across the room at Maggie. Her cheeks were rosy with excitement but she'd handled herself well in the fight. Not a hysterical woman. He liked that. Together they'd be able to keep ahead of the competition.

"Check our things, sweetheart," he ordered. "See if anything is missing."

Margaret did as she'd been told, thinking that hanging around with King was a perilous business. Danger sought him out like a well-aimed arrow. If he hadn't been so quick on his feet, no telling what would have happened. She didn't like the way Arnold's eyes kept following her around the room. He was livid with anger and she had the feeling his mean streak was as thick as his arms. She certainly wished King hadn't riled the man earlier by being so uncharacteristically possessive about her.

Her hands trembling, she sorted through their scattered food packets, candles and extra sets of socks. An inordinately large plastic container of ketchup fell to the floor with a thud. She scooped it up, tossed it back into the bottom of the pack and went on with her inventory. With that much ketchup on hand, she suspected she was in for something less than gourmet meals on the trail.

Everything seemed to be in order until she remembered the book. Hastily she checked around the bed and even under the table. Nothing.

"King, the trapper's diary. It's gone." An irreplaceable museum piece, one with marked trails that corresponded to the treasure map. How would she ever explain the loss to the museum's board of directors? she wondered in dismay.

She watched King's expression close and his lips form a grim line. A sinking feeling knotted in the pit of her stomach. More trouble coming.

"Pack up," he said in a terse command. "We're getting out of here."

"Now?" In the middle of the night? Lord, how had she gotten herself into this mess? "Can't we wait till morning?"

"After that," he said, ignoring her objection, "I want you to find some rope so we can tie these guys up."

That raised a chorus of disapproval from the otherwise quiet skiers who had been watching the action in wide-eyed disbelief.

"Come on, man, you can't do that."

"We're only worried about our money."

"We'll freeze in here."

King yanked Arnold to his feet. "Okay, I'll be a good guy. But only if you promise to keep your buddy under control. We don't want anyone following us." He eyed them carefully. "Is that understood?"

"Hey, yeah, man. We won't let Arnold go no place."

Though King looked skeptical, Margaret was glad he'd given in. With the fire only smoldering, the temperature had already dropped substantially inside the shelter. To leave these men tied up with no way to feed the fire would have been not only cruel but potentially fatal.

She hurried to stuff their belongings back into the pack and snowmobile saddlebags. Then with a quick glance around the cabin to be sure she hadn't forgotten anything, she lifted the pack onto her shoulders and hefted the heavy saddlebags. She staggered under the double weight. "I'm ready." Though she doubted she'd ever be ready for what lay ahead if she stuck with King. Even assuming her back held out.

King gave Arnold a hard shove that landed him in the arms of his friends.

Grabbing her by the hand, King dragged Margaret out the door, slamming it behind them. He took the time to slip a stick through the door latch, neatly blocking an easy pursuit.

Together they raced to the snowmobile, Margaret struggling under the weight of their gear. Dropping the saddlebags across the machine, she leapt on board, wrapping her arms around King's waist as he brought the mechanical monster to life.

When he applied the gas full throttle, her head snapped back.

Lord, she would have been better off staying with the skiers in the shelter. This guy could get her killed.

SHE'D ALWAYS HATED roller-coaster rides. This one was a doozy.

The trail steepened at an alarming rate through a dense stand of lodgepole pines. Caught in the single headlight of the snowmobile, the scenery whizzed by at dizzying speed. Every now and then Margaret caught a quick flash of the trail markers. Based on the jarring sensation in her butt, she decided they were now descending the natural granite staircase that led away from Tuolumne Meadows.

"Why didn't you tell those guys that it was probably Diane who stole their money?" she shouted, forgetting she didn't have to raise her voice to be heard over the muffled noise of the engine.

"What makes you think that?"

"She left the party before we did. Didn't you notice?"

"I only had eyes for you, Maggie girl."

"My name's *Margaret.* I wish you could remember that."

She felt his belly shake with laughter where her arms were wrapped around his waist. Darn him. He knew she didn't like the nickname...except when he said it in that soft, raspy way when they were making love. But she wasn't going to think about that.

"Besides," he pointed out, "what if one of those clowns was in cahoots with her, if indeed she's after the treasure, too? Or maybe someone's working on his own and the whole thievery business was a diversion so we wouldn't notice the missing diary?"

She hadn't considered that possibility and the thought gave her an uncomfortable pause. "Just how many people could have learned about Whitecloud's treasure?''

"Don't know."

"First we had that Smooth-Head Luke character and now you're telling me there could be others?''

"Not more than a dozen. Treasure hunting's a pretty small industry."

Oh, swell. "How do you propose we find that cave without the trapper's diary?" she asked belatedly.

"Not to worry. I made a few notes on the map while you were changing clothes. It's in my pocket."

"Clever of you," she conceded, almost wishing he'd overlooked that small detail so they could forget this whole crazy business.

The ground had leveled and they sailed smoothly over a steel bridge covered with snow. The last vestiges of civilization, she thought. And her last chance to call it quits, turn back and forget this madness. Surely she could find some foundation willing to underwrite the repairs to the museum, if not replace all the exhibits.

Perversely, she didn't want to let go of the chance to find the treasure. Or maybe she simply didn't want to let go of King. She was beginning to actually enjoy riding through the night with him. An exhilarating experience. One that made her feel more alive than she had in years. It was only with King that she could let herself go and fly on eagles' wings like a mythological woman out of time.

Now *that,* she thought with a muffled groan, was a discouraging possibility. You'd think a grown woman would learn not to make the same mistake twice.

Chapter Four

The snowmobile ground up a steep ascent that snaked along the edge of the timberline. Margaret felt herself slipping backward off the machine, her arms too weary to hold her tightly against King's back, a position she'd held for what seemed like hours.

"We've got to stop," she pleaded over the sound of the laboring engine. "Surely we've got a big enough head start so no one will follow us."

"I suppose you're right."

"The moon's almost gone. If we don't stop now, we'll never be able to set up camp." To get a few hours of sleep and have a chance to get warm. At the moment Margaret felt like a slab of meat in a butcher's freezer.

King directed the vehicle off the trail into a stand of silver pines, their silhouettes eerily outlined against the sky. "Did I mention you did good back at the shelter?" he asked.

"I was scared."

"So was I, sweetheart. Most days that's a smart way to be."

In spite of what he'd said, Margaret had the distinct feeling he didn't know the meaning of the word *fear.* "You can be honest with me, King. You're really a reincarnation of Indiana Jones. Right?"

His laughter ringing in her ears warmed her in a way only the unique sound of his voice could. "I'll check the pack for my bullwhip," he joked.

"How can you stand it?" she asked. "People always after you ... or, at least, after the same treasure you are." King seemed to thrive living as close to the abyss as possible. If terror were chocolate, he'd be an addict. Margaret was more comfortable with pasta.

"A little excitement proves you're alive," he pointed out. "The other alternative isn't too swift."

"I've had about all the thrills I can handle for one day, King. I'm ready for a roaring campfire and a whole lot of Zs."

He drew the machine to a halt and switched off the ignition. "I remember a whole lot about you but not your snoring," he commented in a dry, teasing voice.

She blew out a breath that fogged her visor. His references to their prior relationship were decidedly not funny. "If I do, don't you dare wake me."

"Wouldn't think of it, Maggie girl. From my way of thinking, there are much better reasons to wake a woman."

Margaret knew what he was talking about—early mornings together had been some of their most passionate times, interludes she couldn't quite forget no matter how hard she tried.

Gritting her teeth, she conjured up an image of tossing King over a cliff, but decided she was too tired to make the effort. Instead, she dismounted and looked around for a suitable site for their camp. For the zillionth time in the past few hours she wondered if any treasure was worth the stress, then quickly decided the survival of her museum warranted the sacrifice. King owed her. And she owed herself.

"Under those trees looks like a good spot for the tent," she suggested, shrugging off her pack and shifting her aching shoulders. "They'll provide a windbreak."

"You got it, hon."

She watched as King retrieved a bundle from the snowmobile. He paced off the distance between two trees and then tossed the contents of a drawstring sack onto the ground. Aluminum tent poles clattered together onto the snow.

"They told me a five-year-old could put this tent together," King said. The headlight of the snowmobile glinted off the two arced metal tubes he was trying to piece together.

"You did practice setting up the tent, didn't you? I mean, after you bought it?" Margaret shivered in the still, cold air. Her breath formed miniature snowflakes in front of her face.

"They said I wouldn't have any trouble."

"Are there instructions in the bag?"

"Didn't see any. But tents are all pretty much alike." He had one pole hooked over his shoulder with another one stuck between his legs. The two didn't come close to meeting in the middle.

Just like a man, she silently muttered to herself. He'd probably wander around a city lost for hours before asking someone for help.

Margaret checked the bag for directions. Nothing. It figured. Somehow it had been that kind of day.

She picked up a couple of poles and studied them, turning them this way and that. "Are these things supposed to go on the inside or the outside of the tent?"

"Don't know. I asked the guy for a two-man mountaineering tent. I was kind of in a hurry. He said this is the best they make."

"Spare-no-expense King is at it again," she mumbled. She stuck one pole into the other, creating an awkward angle that would have made a terrific tent for a pygmy. "Wasn't there even a picture?"

"Nope. Not that I saw." He dropped the poles onto the snow, stared at them a moment as though they were objects from outer space, then scratched his head. An artless smile canted his lips.

In spite of the cold and her fatigue, Margaret found herself smiling back. King was so easygoing he was impossible not to like. Darn it all.

"Let's start with the tent," he suggested. "Then we can figure out where these things go."

"Remind me not to sign on for an African safari with you as the guide."

He fluffed out the orange fabric like a bed sheet. "Why not? I had a great time in Kenya. Except for the lion attack, of course. That got a little hairy."

Shaking her head, she fought off an urge to laugh. The man was an incorrigible adventurer. No woman could ever hope to tame him. Not that she wanted to try, she assured herself as she grabbed the opposite side of the tent and stretched it across the snow.

She wasn't quite sure how it happened, but a few minutes later she found herself inside the tent with King, twisted like a pretzel, trying to hold one set of tent poles with her feet and another with her mittened hands. "This can't be right," she protested, choking back a giggle.

His situation wasn't much better than hers. He'd practically turned himself inside out in order to reach two corners of the tent at once.

"Come on. We've almost got it now," he insisted. His bravado sounded a bit hollow, given the current shape of the tent.

"This is ridiculous. Here we are, very possibly with a bunch of angry jocks after us, not to mention a crooked ranger and Smooth-Head Luke. The temperature is well below freezing. And we can't even put up a tent."

The flashlight beam caught his face contorted in demonic determination. He grunted. "The guy must have meant a five-year-old *genius*."

Maybe she was suffering from undue fatigue. Or maybe she always felt a bit light-headed around King. At any rate, Margaret collapsed in laughter, and so did the tent, settling across them both in a soft whisper. "I don't think I'm cut out for this." Not at all suited for hanging around with King.

"Maybe I should ask for a refund." King groaned and rolled onto his back.

He lay beside her, gasping with laughter that rumbled up from his chest. His leg pressed against the length of hers. Heat from the contact radiated along her thigh and she tried to block the sensation. She knew how easy it would be to roll over on top of King, crushing him with the kisses she wanted to share and didn't dare think about.

"Can't we just prop this damn thing up and get some sleep?" she pleaded.

He exhaled a long breath and moved away from her, leaving an empty, lonely spot he had once filled. "Guess you're right."

Raking his fingers through his hair, King decided partnering with Maggie was a hell of a strain. Granted, he needed her help to find the treasure, or so he'd told himself, but he didn't like feeling so rattled. For the past half hour he'd been battling a blizzard of sensations, all of them brought on by Maggie's closeness.

Her sultry scent played havoc with his good intentions. Whatever position he chose trying to put up the damn tent, she was there. Her hair spilled over his arm. Her leg draped across his. Her lips were so near it was all he could do not to kiss her and worry about the consequences later. But one kiss would no doubt lead to others. A pleasant thought, of course, yet one filled with obvious dangers, risks he didn't want to take.

"Let's use that longest pole you've got in your hand for the center," he suggested, shifting his thoughts to more practical matters. "Then we'll prop the others at the corners."

Twisting around so her tight little butt was only inches from his hands, she followed his instructions. "I don't think the Boy Scouts are going to give us a merit badge for this mess."

Maybe not, King conceded, but he was likely to get one for self-restraint. In spite of the freezing air, beads of sweat dotted his forehead.

Once they'd made some order out of the chaos, King cleared his throat. He'd had about all the temptation he could handle for one night.

"Let's hit the sack, Maggie girl. It's been a long day." For a moment he contemplated zipping their two sleeping bags together, then thought better of the idea. No sense asking for trouble.

He retrieved the backpack from outside along with the second sleeping bag, dragging them inside while he crawled on his hands and knees. After rolling out the bag, he shrugged off his jacket then zipped down his pants.

"Just what do you think you're doing?" Maggie asked tautly.

"Getting ready for bed." He tugged off his boots.

"Don't you think it would be better if we both kept our clothes on?"

"Why, Maggie," he mocked, "you're not going bashful on me now, are you?"

Even in the light of a single flashlight he saw color creep up her neck. "Well, *I* have no intention of undressing, thank you very much."

Awkwardly he pulled his sweater off over his head. "Suit yourself. Of course, these sleeping bags are good down to zero degrees, which means you'll get too warm, start sweating and then get yourself sick from catching a chill. But if that's what you want . . ."

She scowled at him, visibly weighing the possibility he was lying to her . . . again. After several heartbeats, while King struggled not to smile, she turned her back. Deliberately he watched her peel away her heavy clothing until her slender figure was hidden only by skin-hugging thermal underwear. She hadn't gained an ounce over the years. His fingers itched to circle her midriff just to make sure. But he figured Maggie would not be pleased with his version of scientific investigation.

As she slid into her bag, King shifted his gaze away. His thoughts, however, lingered on the softness of her body, which lay only inches from his. His palms recalled the silken feel of her flesh and the enticing curve of her breasts, the pliable, sensuous contour of her buttocks. Even the golden color of the triangle of hair nestled between her thighs came to mind, and the sweet nectar that lay hidden beyond.

He adjusted his position in the sleeping bag and snapped off the flashlight. It was going to be a hell of a long, uncomfortable night.

Margaret heard him click off the flashlight. Staring into the inky blackness, she tried to steady her heart by taking deep breaths. She knew King had watched her undress. She'd felt his gaze traveling over her like a summer sun. But she hadn't dared look over her shoulder to confirm her suspicions.

Maybe she'd only been imagining it, she told herself.

The reality of her situation was difficult enough to deal with. She and King were crammed into the out-of-kilter space, lying much closer to each other than Margaret would have liked. She heard his breathing close to her ear and caught his musky, masculine scent.

She forced herself to concentrate on getting warm, and as she did her mind drifted to the time she and King had stood on a cliff overlooking the New Mexico desert, watching the setting sun cast purple-and-blue shadows across the landscape. The colors were vivid in her memory. What had once seemed barren, an unending panorama of beige, had taken on new texture and vitality with King holding her in his arms.

"I DIDN'T KNOW THE DESERT could be so beautiful," Margaret whispered, awed by both the scenery and the man who held her.

"Wait till you see the dawn." King's seductive voice and the soft kiss he placed on her temple were filled with the promise of tomorrow. "With me."

Sweet anticipation, as warm as the desert breeze teasing across her bare shoulders, fluttered within her. "We'll have to search the ruins to the north tomorrow."

"We'll wake up early. Assuming we get any sleep at all." His palms slid slowly over her buttocks and cupped her against the nest of his hips. The light covering of hair on his thighs brushed against her flesh below the line of her cutoff shorts. The slight roughness sensitized every nerve ending at the point of contact.

"I'd like to try some excavations in the ceremonial room."

"I can think of more enjoyable ways to spend the day."

So could Margaret. In spite of the warm air, a shivery sensation trailed across her flesh. Her mouth felt parched and she thirsted for what she sensed King could provide.

His cotton shirt hung open, inviting her intimate investigation. Unbidden, her hands explored King's broad chest, furred with a trace of curly hair that arrowed past the waistband of his khaki shorts. "The museum paid for my trip. A summer job. I really should—"

"All in due time, Maggie girl." His hands shifted to her midriff, spanning the strip of flesh bared by her halter top. His thumbs nestled at the swell of her breasts, lifting gently with a tantalizing promise of more to come. A circle of heat started right where he touched her, growing more intense by the moment, radiating outward like a miniature sun. The rays flowed through her limbs.

She drew a shaky breath. Except for a few unsatisfying encounters, Margaret had had little experience with men. Certainly none with a man quite so thoroughly masculine as King. For once in her life she didn't want to think about her work, her specialty in American Indians. She simply wanted to feel. Feminine. Desirable. All those things King had made her feel since they had first met among these ancient ruins. At this particular moment she couldn't recall if their meeting had been only yesterday or an eternity ago. In all the ways that mattered she felt she had been biding her time until King entered her life.

Still, things seemed to be moving much too fast. This urgent need for a man wasn't her usual style.

With belated awareness Margaret realized King had been seducing her from the very first moment. As they had worked together excavating sample areas in the ruins, their bodies had touched in a way that was entirely too well orchestrated—his hand casually at the small of her back, a muscular thigh brushing against hers, the way he had wiped a smudge of dirt from her cheek. His laughter and appreciative smiles had deceived her. Or perhaps she had simply wanted to fall under his spell.

As the waning sun cast deepening shadows, Margaret's senses seemed extraordinarily alert. She heard the faintest whisper of wind through the low scrub growth at the edge of the cliff and caught the tangy scent of creosote on the air. In the distance a coyote called to the rising moon.

She placed her lips on King's chest, tasting the salt of his body. His heart pounded with the same heavy beat she experienced within her own chest, an echo of the visceral attraction that had them both on the edge. As she felt the nub of his nipple grow taut from her ministrations, she heard him moan and smiled to herself. She'd never felt so free, so uninhibited. So recklessly bold.

"Maggie girl, I hope you know what you're doing." He spoke in a low, raspy voice that shimmered down her spine. He wanted her—of that she could be quite confident.

"I'm sure what I don't know, you'll be willing to teach me." There was much she wanted to learn from King. The feeling of sweat-slicked bodies perfectly in tune reaching a peak together. The knowledge of all of her erotic zones intimately explored by an expert.

His eyes looked nearly indigo in the fading light. "I suspect you'll be an *A*-plus student."

"I hope you'll assign lots of homework," she teased with a reckless abandon she'd never before experienced.

"I plan to insist on a great deal of private tutoring."

He framed her face with his palms, lowering his mouth to cover hers. At first the kiss was gentle, then grew more demanding until she was breathless, her heart rate accelerating with each thrust of his tongue. She parried in eager response, his unique flavor an aphrodisiac.

His expert fingers released her halter top and it slid to the ground with a sibilant sound. She stood in the moonlight for his careful perusal, feeling her flesh heat with his approval. Her breasts had never felt so full, her nipples so eager to be caressed. Sensual awareness curled through her body and throbbed low in her belly.

"Perfect," he said, his voice heavy with masculine praise. He lowered his head to suckle first one nipple then the other, as though he totally understood her needs without a word being spoken. His tongue swirled around the areola in a soft, heated caress.

The aching need in her breasts sent a ripple of weakness to her knees. She clung to his shoulders to steady herself. "King, could we..." She drew another shuddering breath as his teeth raked tenderly against her sensitive flesh. "Please..." The urge Margaret felt was as primitive as the ancient peoples who had once lived in the ruins she and King had explored all day. And far more compelling.

"Let's get off this ledge," he suggested, his voice filled with husky undertones.

Taking her hand, he led her inside the crumbling ruins, quickly stripping her shorts off to join his on the dusty ground. The rock walls had held in the heat of the day but felt cool compared to the banked fires King had ignited within her.

The sight of his strong, tanned body gave her a sense of unabashed pleasure. Muscles rippled across his flat stomach and her gaze was drawn to his magnificent arousal. Though she knew her total admiration of his masculine body was uncharacteristically bold, she didn't even consider looking away. She'd never known simply admiring a man would bring her such hedonistic satisfaction.

He laid her down on an Indian blanket, the coarse weave on her back mimicking the roughened texture of his hands as he caressed her body—her breasts, the tender skin across her abdomen, along the inner seam of her thighs and finally to their apex. She shifted restlessly beneath his hands, hands that knew her pleasure points even better than she knew them herself.

"Kiss me, King," she pleaded. Her fingers wove themselves through the thick waves of his hair and she pulled him close.

"For as often and as long as you want," he promised. "Wherever you want."

"Everywhere," she admitted, surprised by the truth of her statement.

Slowly, with excruciating attention to detail, he did as she had requested. The warmth of his lips, his textured tongue, tasted the column of her neck, the welcoming indentation at the base of her throat. He visited each spot with lazy languor and then moved on to the sensitive flesh at the bend of her elbow, along her midriff, moving inexorably lower until he reached the excited nub of her womanhood.

As he worked his magic, Margaret was aware of the continuum of life, the reenactment of ageless movements between man and woman. She was one with King, and he with her. An aura of variegated light and heat surrounded them. Brilliant. Radiating from deep within Margaret until it encompassed all thought and sensation.

THAT SAME FIERY AFTERGLOW still lingered when Margaret woke to cold mountain air biting her cheeks and faint morning light filtering through the tangle of orange tent fabric.

Disoriented, Margaret knew she was no longer in New Mexico but somewhere much colder. Yet the muscular arms that held her in sleep, and the broad shoulder on which her head rested, were the same. *The very same,* she realized with a start.

Lord, how had that happened? she wondered with rising panic. They were still in separate sleeping bags, but just barely. Somehow in the night she'd found warmth in King's arms when she should have stayed on her own darn side of the tent.

New Mexico had been a foolish interlude—and she vowed not to repeat it in the Sierra high country.

Extricating herself from King's arms, however, would be no easy task. Not without waking him. And the last thing she wanted was for him to know how intimately they'd been cuddling during the night.

His arm was looped firmly around her back, his hand unerringly resting on the curve of her breast. Through her thermal underwear she felt his firm grip. If he hadn't been breathing so easily she would have sworn he knew exactly what he was about. But then, even in sleep, seduction was probably on King's mind. She'd simply have to remove the offending hand and edge back to her own side of the tent.

Cautiously she lifted her head from his shoulder. If she moved with enough care—

A sound outside the tent stopped her in midmovement. A snap of a twig. An unnatural rustling of branches.

"King!" She whispered his name and sat up abruptly.

His eyes popped open.

"There's someone outside the tent," she said.

"You're imagining—"

"No, I'm not. I heard him. He can't be more than ten feet away."

That news brought a scowl to King's face. "You sure?"

"What if it's Crazy Arnold and his friends? Or worse, Smooth-Head Luke?"

King tried to rouse himself from the very pleasant dream he'd been enjoying. Rubbing his palm along his whiskered jaw, he decided the possibility of an intruder was all too real.

"See if you can find the hunting knife in the backpack," he ordered.

"Don't you have a gun?"

In spite of her whisper King heard a good deal of strain in Maggie's voice. He also noted she looked sexy as hell in her skintight long johns with her hair nicely tousled from sleep. Too bad the dream hadn't been real.

"People can get hurt with guns," he said.

Something, or someone, bumped against the tent, shaking the fabric.

"Oh, God..." Margaret groaned, yanking gear out of the pack and tossing it aside. "I can't find the damn thing!"

"The knife ought to be in the side pocket." King reached past her to help in the search, his arm brushing against the familiar shape of her breast. Some dreams were more vivid than others, he concluded.

"I've got it!" Triumphantly she held up a ... metal can opener? Her face fell.

"Not quite, sweetheart, but at least it has a sharp point." He took the opener from her. Not much of a weapon but it might have to do, though King didn't relish the thought of battling Little John with anything less than a sledgehammer. "Keep looking."

A dark, ominous shadow moved across the tent. Anxiety drew the moisture from King's mouth and he forced a calmness he didn't necessarily feel.

"King! What are we going to do? We're trapped."
She gave him a wild-eyed look before returning to the
search.

Heavy breathing, combined with a low, rumbling
sound, came from King's side of the tent. He crouched
into a defensive position, gripping the can opener in
his sweaty palm.

"Just stay behind me, sweetheart. I'll take care of
it." His gaze darted from one side of the tent to the
other. Whoever was out there was doing a hell of a lot
of moving around. And he was big, too, based on the
shadow. About ten feet tall. "Back off!" he warned.
"I'm armed." Sort of.

The tent shook. With a sound that put teeth on
edge, the nylon fabric began to tear.

Maggie screamed.

Chapter Five

King lunged at the intruder.

Sharp claws flashed through the gaping hole, ripping at his shoulders and arms. Snarling growls punctuated each thrusting attack.

"What the hell!" King shouted.

Paralyzed by terror, Margaret watched thick, fur-covered forelegs and black paws take swipe after swipe at King. The animal's bearlike head followed his every effort to dodge the sharp claws. Huge teeth snapped at the air. An evil scent permeated the tent and another piercing snarl rumbled in fierce warning.

"Find the damn knife!"

King's order jolted Margaret out of her stupor. Upending the backpack, she dumped all the remaining gear onto her sleeping bag. Food. Rope. Extra clothing. Finally the knife appeared, sheathed in a leather holder.

With shaking hands she grabbed up the weapon, brandishing it in the air, only to be halted by the sight of King locked in a death grip with the wolverine. She tried to find an opening to stab at the animal.

On her knees she edged around the tent to get a better angle of attack. There was little room to maneuver. All of it was dangerous territory, all of it within reach of sharp claws and pointed teeth.

And wherever she moved, King was in the way. She didn't dare risk plunging the knife forward for fear she'd kill King instead of the beast.

"Let him go!" she screamed. "I've got the knife."

King muttered a curse.

Almost as though the animal sensed the new threat, it flew at Margaret. She took an ineffectual swing with the knife just as King latched on to the scruff of its neck.

Snarls, shouts and screams filled the tent. Fur flew. Cloth ripped. Bodies tumbled and bumped against each other. Claws flashed.

With an enormous amount of strength King lifted the creature by the back of its neck and heaved it out the way it had come in. It landed with a thud against a tree trunk.

The animal yelped in pain, gave one more deep snarl and raced away from the tent, its body low to the ground, its forepaw held in the air.

"Oh, my God," Margaret gasped. Her pulse ticked a wild beat at her throat and her chest heaved with the effort to catch her breath. The knife slipped from her hand.

"What the hell was that?" King asked, his breath coming as rapidly as hers. "I thought bears hibernated during the winter."

"Wolverines don't. And that's what we just tangled with. The meanest animal around, pound for pound. They're practically extinct in the Sierras."

"I could do with one less right about now, I'll tell you. Forget endangered species." His elbow propped on one bent knee, he rested his head in his hand. Sweat edged down his jaw. "That was one hell of a wake-up call."

Margaret's hand reached out to smooth his mussed hair but she withdrew, afraid of the sensations that made her want to hold King in her arms. She'd been so frightened, so terrified that King would be killed by the rampaging wolverine, that her only thoughts had been for his safety. The press of tears pooled in her eyes. God, she didn't want him to die.

Through her blurred focus her gaze settled on King's shoulder. An ugly reddish brown stain seeped through his thermal shirt. Fear constricted her throat once again.

"King, you're hurt." Her words were no more than a hoarse whisper.

"I'm okay." He shrugged off her concern. "I've gotta make sure that damn animal is long gone."

Standing, he peered through the rip in the tent. Golden sunlight touched his hair, streaking it with highlights of red and yellow to mix with the brown. The clear blue sky outlined his broad shoulders. From waist to calf his long johns accented his rounded butt and lean yet powerful physique. Muscular thighs rode above well-shaped calves that begged for a woman's caress.

A magnificent male of the species, ready to do hand-to-hand combat with a savage animal to protect Margaret. She gave no thought at all to the futile effort she'd made to ward off the attack. It had been King who had saved the day...and saved her, with his strength and ferocity.

A feeling very much like love rose in her chest. She fought the sensation, pressing it painfully back into that tiny spot where she'd kept it hidden from herself all these years. If she admitted, even for a moment, that she still cared for King, it would be like unstopping a cork in a champagne bottle that had traveled a very bumpy road.

"Why the hell did that animal attack us?" King asked. "Seems like he'd give humans a wide berth."

"I don't know. Maybe he smelled our food and was hungry. Or maybe it's mating season. Males can get pretty aggressive in the spring."

"So you figure we were victims of raging hormones?"

"Possibly. Sit down, King," she said, reaching for the first-aid kit. "Let me tend your wounds."

"He just barely grazed me."

"Don't be so macho. The cuts will get infected if we don't clean them."

He squatted down on his haunches.

"Off with your shirt," she ordered.

He gave her a quick, appraising look, his eyes sparking with a mix of relief and the gleam of teasing laughter. "I'd been hoping you'd ask."

Ignoring the sudden flutter in her belly, she returned a don't-give-me-that look. "This is going to hurt you more than it does me," she responded with a fair amount of tartness. She dribbled some antiseptic on a piece of gauze as he pulled his shirt off over his head.

A dozen bloody claw marks crisscrossed his shoulders and extended down one arm. Fortunately, none of them appeared too deep. Because of King's strength and bravery, she'd been left unscathed.

He sucked in a quick breath at the first brush of cloth against the longest gash, then evened his breathing into a steady rhythm. Margaret knew it cost him plenty not to wince each time she cleansed a new wound. She worked diligently in spite of the raging emotions that buffeted her from every side.

To actually touch King's bare flesh was a sweet tempest Margaret simply had to endure. A familiar smattering of freckles covered his shoulders; muscles flexed across his back when he moved. Though his skin was smooth, every inch was decidedly masculine. He was the kind of man a woman wanted to caress, often and intimately. Margaret's fingers itched to do just that.

Again and again she tried to shift her thoughts to other matters. Reality intruded like a hot spell in the middle of winter, welcome but potentially dangerous, thinning the ice barrier she'd so carefully constructed around her heart.

This was the man who'd left her alone in a Santa Fe hotel room, the rent paid, an airline ticket back home on the dresser. But no note. Not so much as an adios. She'd felt cheap and used and hurt beyond words.

Why, when she had gloried in their newfound relationship, had he left so abruptly? *So heartlessly.* Did she dare ask the question that had been plaguing her for nearly five years?

She swallowed uncomfortably. Damn it all. She deserved an answer.

"You left Santa Fe in a big hurry." Her calm voice belied the churning in the pit of her stomach. "Why the rush?"

His long, tapered fingers closed around her wrist and his thumb stroked gently against the rapid beat of her pulse. He held her gaze for a dozen counts, his eyes darkening with what could have been taken for desire.

"I'm sorry, Maggie girl. I felt the trap closing. You wouldn't have wanted that."

Trap? Is that what he thought of love? "I never said anything about commitment." She'd never had a chance.

"You didn't have to."

"I gather you thought the airline ticket represented payment in full for services rendered?" The memory still had the power to bring a bitter taste to her mouth.

"God, no, Maggie. I never meant it that way. I knew you were broke and I didn't want to leave you stranded."

"Very thoughtful of you." She considered pouring the entire bottle of stinging antiseptic over his head but figured that would be a wasted effort. "I came close to tearing up the ticket and taking the bus."

"But you didn't?"

"No. Instead, I upgraded to first-class and had them charge your account." She tilted her chin. "I decided I was worth more than cattle-car class."

With an amused smile he said, "You are, indeed, Maggie girl. Worth a thousand times more." He shifted his grip from her wrist to her left hand, folding his fingers around hers. "I figured by now you'd have found someone else. No ring?"

She tried to pull away but he didn't release her. "I've been seeing a gentleman."

"Gentleman?" He raised his eyebrows. "That sounds incredibly boring."

"Robert is very nice. He's a sixth-grade teacher, a widower, and he has two lovely children who are the apple of his eye. He's settled," she insisted with a defensive twist of her jaw. "He has a good, solid future. A woman could do worse."

"A woman like you would go bonkers in two weeks."

"You don't know anything about me, Kingsley McDermott." Except that it was true Robert didn't generate a single spark that came close to what she'd felt for King—however foolishly her heart had misled her. "Robert is exactly what I'm looking for." As far from a dreamer as she could get.

"Are you sleeping with him?"

"That is none of your damn business." No way was Margaret going to admit she'd shared only a few uninspiring kisses with Robert in all the months they'd been seeing each other. It was no one's concern except her own.

King's expletive was decidedly ungallant.

She whirled, grabbed up some bandages and plastered them on his wounds as best as her shaking hands could manage. She didn't even care when he winced. Inside, she was hurting too much. She'd asked her question and gotten an answer. The only result was a painful return to reality. King didn't want to be *trapped*.

KING WALKED WELL AWAY from the campsite to answer the call of nature. He also needed a few minutes to think.

He hadn't meant to hurt Maggie, but that had certainly been the result of his hasty departure from Santa Fe. Though her chin had been lifted at a stubborn angle as she told him she'd upgraded the airline ticket, he'd seen the reflection of pain in her eyes. Gutsy lady. She hadn't wanted him to know the truth.

She'd never be able to guess how much he'd wanted to stay. Or the number of times he'd been tempted to search her out in LA.

But he couldn't bring that much misery down on any woman—most especially a woman like Maggie.

King had known since he was a kid that marriage was out of the question for him. He could never put a wife through the torment his parents had suffered. Trapping a woman into a life that would put her in a virtual prison was totally unacceptable. He'd never regretted the necessity for that decision more than he did at this very moment.

The sins of his father—or, more accurately, the man's success—were a heavy burden King couldn't shed. The wealth he'd inherited shackled him to a past he didn't want and had spent years trying to avoid.

Why the hell had his brother had to die, anyway?

In every direction King looked, mountains rose to jagged, granite-scarred peaks, blocking his view in the same way his past had limited his options for the future. A jet contrail and a few harmless clouds drifted silently across the morning sky, casting shadows that moved in a lazy pattern over the glistening snow. Through some quirk of refraction, a column of sunlight created a cylinder around a single pine. It was an odd illusion, almost as if the tree had been set afire in a dazzling display of gold. The strange sight was accompanied by the distinctive rattle of Indian beads.

The short hairs rose on the back of King's neck. It couldn't be . . .

Wind-twisted branches took on a new appearance as he watched, dumbfounded. Like a hidden picture, the outline of a face emerged from what had once been simply a tree. The features shaped themselves into a nose and eyes, a wrinkled face that was as familiar to King as his own.

He drew a quick breath. The altitude must be getting to him, he decided, held motionless as he stared at the image of his friend Whitecloud.

"Have you not yet found the treasure you seek?" asked the illusion.

No way was King going to respond to a figment of his imagination.

Instead, he glanced back the way he had come. The tent was still visible, as was Maggie, who was standing near the tent. Everything looked perfectly normal.

Except, when King shifted his gaze to the tree again, Whitecloud's weather-lined face still hovered among the branches. It gave King an unsettling feeling in his gut.

"The treasure you seek was once within your grasp," the image persisted, "and yet it eluded you. Few men are given a second chance."

As absurd as it seemed, King felt a need to respond to his longtime mentor. After all these years he had some feeling the Indian did indeed have powers beyond his own understanding. He could only hope Maggie didn't hear him talking to a tree. As a rule that wasn't his style. He'd certainly never thought of himself as superstitious.

"I don't know what you're talking about, old man. We aren't anywhere near the cave marked on your map. And I don't know why I'm hearing your voice. So why don't you just bug off." Forget that it hurt to see his friend again and know it was only a reflection of how much he missed the man's wisdom as a part of his life.

The image wavered as though a sympathetic breeze had touched the pine limbs, and the sound of beads was there again. "The Great Spirit has not yet finished with me."

Terrific. Now King was in the middle of one of Whitecloud's visions. And he hadn't even been chewing dried leaves. "Some guy with a rifle sure wanted you out of the way. Do you know who shot you?"

"That has not been revealed to me. But it is of little consequence."

"It might not matter to you, but it does to me—if the guy is still after the gold coins. I don't want to be his next target." Or have Maggie in his sights, either.

"I will do my best to protect you, but my powers are limited."

"That's not very encouraging."

"You have many resources to help you overcome a threat from others. It is the threat from within that troubles me."

Whitecloud had always spoken in riddles, even when he was alive. King concluded that, like growing old, being dead didn't change a man's basic personality. "What the heck do you mean by that?"

"When you claim the treasure, you will understand."

"Come on, old man, you can't leave me hanging like this." But it was too late to argue. With the shifting winds, the cylinder of light dissolved like pinpricks of snow shaken from the tree. The hairs on the back of King's neck relaxed.

Cautiously he approached the silver pine. As far as he could detect, it was just like every other tree that clung to the mountainside. No hidden camera. No magician's gimmicks.

He broke off a clump of five needles and crushed them between his fingers until he caught the distinctive scent of pine. No illusion there. Yet a moment ago he'd certainly been hallucinating.

Whitecloud's appearance had shaken King more than he cared to admit. Losing your wits while tramping around a wilderness area in freezing weather wasn't a good idea. He'd have to watch himself.

LEANING AGAINST the snowmobile, Margaret ate her breakfast of instant oatmeal. The sharp crags and peaks of Yosemite struck her as both beautiful and starkly impersonal. It was a monochromatic world, highlighted only by an endless sky. There was no warmth in these rugged mountains. She had the uncomfortable feeling her life was equally lacking in those things that she really wanted. Someone to share both the emotional peaks and valleys that are a part of living. An excitement about facing each new day. Love.

She wondered if she would ever find that kind of relationship. With a large dose of self-honesty, she doubted Robert would add much color to her life, however kind and steady a man he might be.

With a sigh she stirred the mush in the dish and dreamed about something exciting for breakfast— maybe like the flaming crepes she'd had with King in Santa Fe. No, she didn't want to think about that morning and all that had preceded their breakfast in bed.

At the sound of King's footsteps in the snow she looked up. Dressed in black, he created a striking image as he made his way toward her across the stark landscape. Powerful. In charge. And frighteningly attractive.

If only she'd known she would be seeing King again, perhaps she could have prepared herself. A little self-hypnosis might have helped . . . like repeating ten thousand times a day *I am not attracted to six-foot-tall men with wavy brown hair, mocking blue eyes and cocky grins.*

It simply wasn't fair that she had fallen once for a man who was so blatantly wrong for her, and was on the verge of making the same damn mistake again.

"You've been gone awhile," she said, suppressing an unwelcome shudder of desire. Somehow she had to get over her instant and heated reaction to the man.

"I had some thinking to do." He knelt by the one-burner stove she'd perched on a rock, poured a helping of instant oatmeal in a bowl and added boiling water. "Anything unusual going on around here?"

Just a little soul-searching of her own. "No. Everything's quiet."

"No sign of the wolverine?"

"He'll probably stay away now. I'm sure you scared him to death with that can opener."

"Hope so." He gave her a lopsided grin that made her heart constrict, then she watched as he spooned some cereal into his mouth, amazed at how fascinated she was with the movements of his lips. "You boil a mean pot of water, Ms. Townsend. Do you include domestic talents among your skills?"

"I'm a pretty fair cook," she conceded. Not that it was likely King would ever find out for himself. Camping offered few opportunities to demonstrate her culinary abilities, and they'd both been content with room service in Santa Fe.

She only wished she weren't drawn to King so strongly. His eyes, and the way he looked at her, were the most difficult to resist. Something about that sil-

ver-blue color and the sparkle of mischief that so often lurked in their depths had addictive qualities. The
crinkles that formed at the corners when he squinted
into the sun simply added to her feeling of drugged
intoxication. The FDA ought to label Kingsley Mc-
Dermott as hazardous to a woman's peace of mind.

She wondered with a wrenching sensation in her
chest if he'd abandoned a whole string of women in
assorted hotel rooms, or if that special treatment had
been hers alone. Deciding the answer to her question
didn't matter, she finished the last of her tasteless
oatmeal.

"Let's take a look at the map," King said as he set
his bowl aside. He had the most powerful urge to draw
the back of his fingers across Maggie's cheek. She
didn't have on a smidgen of makeup. Her rosy glow
was entirely natural, the cold air kissing her cheeks just
as King would like to do himself.

Her hair hung loosely across her shoulders and he
watched as she flicked it back out of the way in an
artless, sexy-as-hell gesture. His stomach muscles
clenched and those that were a bit lower did a number
on him, too. Damn, he wanted the woman.

"Wish we still had the trapper's diary," Margaret
said, feeling her body heat under King's intense gaze
and suspecting she knew just what he was thinking
about—the same subject that had been all too much
on her mind, as well.

"We'll manage without getting lost." He pulled the
map from his inside coat pocket and spread it out on
the rock. Margaret joined him, trying not to get too
close while still being able to see the markings on the

map. Even so, she caught his masculine scent and her heart thudded an extra beat.

"The best I can tell, we're still on the Pacific Crest Trail, right about here," she said, pointing to a spot south of Virginia Canyon, noted on the Indian map as a series of sharp peaks and valleys. "The trail's well marked and heavily traveled in the summer. Very likely it's a route the Miwoks used. I think we ought to stay on it until we get near Piute Mountain."

"Sounds reasonable. Then we can circle south into this area where the cave is supposed to be." He showed her on the map the direction he was thinking about.

A distant rumble caused Margaret to lift her head. "What's that noise?" she asked. Except for a few scattered clouds, the sky was a clear blue. Certainly there was no sign of an approaching thunderstorm.

"I don't know. Maybe it's just the wind."

"I don't think so." She placed her hand on his arm. "It could be an engine, King. Like the motor of a snowmobile."

Listening, he cocked his head. "Our friendly ranger?"

"Or the jocks. Arnold didn't look like the forgiving type." Anxiety drove Margaret to her feet and she brushed the snow from the back of her trousers. "Let's get packed. I'm not in the mood to entertain visitors just now."

King agreed.

The tent came down much more easily than it had gone up. Within minutes they had stowed their gear in the snowmobile and Margaret had hefted the backpack onto her shoulders, mounting the vehicle behind King.

Taking a deep breath, she wrapped her arms around him. It was going to be another long, stress-filled day. Next time—if she was ever foolish enough to do this again—she'd demand her own snowmobile.

NOT FAR FROM THEIR campsite the trail leveled to run through an expansive stand of red fir Christmas trees, their spiny branches wrapped with short needles that almost looked blue. Though Margaret didn't see any wildlife, occasional telltale footprints revealed that not all of the local inhabitants slept away the winter in some warm burrow.

At one point a rosy finch dipped low above them, as though on an inspection tour of the noisy intruders to his silent domain. When he circled, then lifted his wings toward the highest peaks, Margaret's heart filled with a sense of wonder.

In spite of herself she wrapped her arms more tightly around King's waist. In return he covered her hands with one of his. Her chest expanded with an upwelling of love. No man was more adept at providing her with memorable moments.

Something about the vastness of the land gave Margaret a strange sense of intimacy with King. Never had she felt quite so dependent—quite so vulnerable—with any man. No doubt the fact that their bodies were molded solidly against one another was a large part of the cause.

Minutes and hours melted together with only brief interludes for rest and a chance to eat a little trail mix.

Then they were roaring across the starkly beautiful landscape again, as though they were not two separate people but two who had become one.

The trail steepened to a series of precipitous switchbacks. Margaret felt herself leaning left into the wall of snow that brushed against her shoulder, avoiding the yawning abyss that threatened only inches away on the opposite side.

To her surprise and relief, King halted the snowmobile.

"What's wrong?" she asked, lifting her head to look over his shoulder.

"The trail's blocked. Looks like an avalanche."

A wide swath of upended trees had careered down the hillside in a tumble of snow that left boulders resting on top of the debris. Margaret shuddered. The destructive power must have been an awesome thing to witness. "Maybe that's the noise we heard this morning," she suggested.

"Could be." King dismounted and removed his helmet. For a moment he studied the terrain, his fingers raking through his sweat-darkened hair. "As avalanches go, this wasn't a big one. I think we can work our way down and around it."

"What makes you an instant expert on avalanches?"

"I ran across a couple in the Andes."

"The *Andes?*"

"Sure. I was there in eighty-seven. Then again a couple of years after that."

She shook her head in amazement. "Is there anywhere on this earth you haven't traveled?"

Canting her a lopsided grin that made Margaret's heart tick an extra beat, he said, "I've never been to the South Pole. Want to come with me?"

"Thanks for the invitation, but I'll pass." If Margaret got out of the Sierras in one piece, and with her heart still intact, she'd consider herself fortunate. "Has it occurred to you that if we mess around here too much, we could start a new avalanche? This all looks pretty unstable to me."

"That's why we're going to push the snowmobile across the slide area."

"Push?" she echoed. "This machine must weigh a ton."

"About that."

He said it so casually all Margaret could do was sputter her objection. "There is another option, you know. We could go back."

Shocked surprise lifted his eyebrows.

"Those gold coins have been hidden up here for more than a hundred years," she persisted. "Surely they can wait till summer." That would give Margaret time to rethink this entire expedition . . . or invest in a one-way ticket for King to the South Pole.

"Wouldn't want to give Smooth-Head Luke a chance to figure out where the gold is, would you?"

"Maybe I could get him to donate it to the museum," she muttered as she slid her aching body off the snowmobile. "Everybody needs a tax write-off."

King's warm laughter rippled across the harsh landscape and curled back into a spot in Margaret's heart that had been empty for a long time. Damn it all.

Why did King, of all people, have the power to lift her spirits, or send them plummeting into the depths, with just the sound of his voice?

Sinking knee-deep in snow with every step, Margaret shoved at the back of the snowmobile. King did the same up front, steering along a course that was anything but level. One wrong move and they, plus a million tons of snow, would likely be at the bottom of the ravine. The very thought dried Margaret's mouth.

In contrast, King hummed softly to himself.

The man was enough to drive any woman crazy.

She pushed and grunted, her breath coming in painful gulps. The altitude, along with so much physical effort, was really getting to her. King hardly seemed to be building up a sweat, while she felt a river of perspiration edging down her face. Darn him for being in such good shape.

As she recalled, he had a lot of stamina when it came to lovemaking, too. In that case, however, she'd pretty well held her own.

With a final shove from them both, the snowmobile lurched onto the trail again.

Panting from the exertion, Margaret collapsed right where she was. Her chest heaved. Her body felt drained of every molecule of oxygen. With her arms and legs lacking the energy to budge another step, she rolled onto her back and looked up into King's silver-blue eyes. An unwelcome surge of adrenaline—or was it simply lust?—kicked up her already rapid heart rate.

"You're in terrific shape, Maggie girl. Didn't think you were going to make it there for a minute."

She groaned. "I'm going to die. And it's all your fault."

He removed his gloves and palmed her face, his hands warm on her cheeks. "I wouldn't want that to happen. Not ever."

The raspy timbre of his voice wore an intimate path right through Margaret's weakened defenses. She watched helplessly as King's eyes darkened with unconcealed desire and his head lowered toward hers.

She remembered. Lord, she remembered the persuasive feel of King's lips on hers, their gentle persistence, his distinctive flavor—sweet and intoxicating. Any protest she might have mounted melted as the heat of his mouth crossed hers with the familiar possessiveness of a returning lover. The icy years of hurt and regret thawed like a river in spring, breaking loose from their banks and sending currents raging in a maelstrom of forgotten pleasure. This was King. *Her* King. All of her recollections, so vivid a moment ago, dimmed in comparison to the new reality of his kiss.

His fingers shifted through her hair and he cradled her head in his palm. The flick of his tongue across the seam of her lips sent ripples of heat through her body. Not before she'd met King, or since he'd left her, had Margaret felt like this. She drew a deep, shuddering breath, and as her lips parted his tongue slid between them. The velvet tip explored the tender flesh of her mouth, renewing an old acquaintanceship in exquisite detail.

Eagerly Margaret began a quest of her own. The tip of his tongue. Straight, even teeth. Masculine nectar she drank in with the same urgency a starving man would have approached a banquet.

With a muffled groan he drew back, his face hovering close enough so Margaret could feel the warmth of his breath on her flushed cheeks, riding across her features in short, choppy gasps.

"I've missed you, Maggie girl," he said in a low voice that was as choked with emotion as Margaret's heart.

"You probably haven't given me a single thought since Santa Fe." While memories of King had never been far from her mind, however much she might like to claim otherwise.

"Not true. I've never forgotten you."

His admission tightened in a band of hope around her chest. "You never . . . tried to find me."

With his fingertips he combed back strands of her hair that had fallen across her face. "I thought about it dozens of times. Sometimes in the oddest places, like down in some stinking mine shaft, or on top of a mountain. But I didn't dare try to contact you."

"Why on earth not?"

His bark of laughter had a brittle sound, like the shattering of dreams. "Because I'm poison for a woman like you, sweetheart. Deadly."

A new pain cut through Margaret, ripping at old wounds that had never fully healed. She turned her head and slid away from his grasp.

"Then I guess we'd better get on with this expedition so we can get it over with." Ignoring how the cold air brought sudden tears to her eyes, Margaret levered herself upright. With a determined gesture she hefted the backpack from the back of the snowmobile, pulled her helmet on over her head, snapped the visor closed and straddled the machine. "Let's go."

Chapter Six

Only the mountain peaks still held the sunlight when King pulled off the trail again. It was one of the few spots beside the trail wide enough to accommodate their camp in the rugged area. All along their route, granite cliffs too steep to hold a snowflake had alternated with towering cornices teetering on the brink of collapse.

Silent shadows blanketed the landscape with an eerie blue tint. Above the timberline, an occasional coney, looking for all the world like a guinea pig, darted among the rock piles or bleated a warning to others from a high rock perch. Once an alpine rabbit had fled from the path of the snowmobile.

Margaret's body ached with bruises from riding all day. Her ego was equally blue and battered. Why the devil couldn't she resist King? He'd made it abundantly clear his only interest in her, outside of getting her help to find the treasure, was a full dose of lust. She should have known better than to allow even one kiss.

He halted the machine. Gratefully, Margaret dismounted and stretched.

"Let me have your backpack," he offered. "It must be getting pretty heavy by now."

Like three or four tons on her back, but she wasn't going to admit that. It was important that she not become totally dependent on King. "I can manage."

He eyed her speculatively for a moment, then shrugged. "Whatever you say."

With a few quick motions he unleashed the tent from the back of the snowmobile. Without further comment he carried the bundle to a sheltered spot among snow-covered boulders.

Margaret wondered what he was thinking about. Sex and gold coins, she imagined. Hardly the makings for a scintillating evening's conversation around a campfire, much less a reliable foundation for a long-term relationship.

With a sigh she followed him. If everything went reasonably well, by tomorrow they'd be at the cave, she reminded herself. Then two more days and she'd be home with funds to repair the museum and, with luck, even expand the exhibits. Unfortunately, the price she'd pay would be three days of nervous tension. A dismaying thought.

Particularly since her experiences with King had never gone quite as she'd planned.

Just as she bent to straighten the corner of the tent King had tossed onto the ground, a shot rang through the still air, echoing from peak to valley.

The impact of the bullet drove Margaret to her knees.

More trouble, she thought with a groan. Three more days hanging around with King might well exceed her life expectancy.

At the crack of the rifle shot, King launched himself at Maggie, tumbling her onto the ground and rolling her behind the protection of a snow-clad boulder. Half dragging, half carrying her, he hauled her toward safety.

"King!" She choked out his name so painfully it tore at his gut.

"Hang on, sweetheart."

A terrifying, sickly sweet stickiness covered his palm. He swore under his breath. She'd been hit. The son of a—! Somebody had tried to kill his Maggie!

Another bullet whined over their heads.

King shouldn't have brought Maggie along on this trip. It had only been an excuse to see her, he realized with guilty, though belated, awareness. He could have found the treasure on his own. He didn't need to risk Maggie's life. Cursing himself six ways from Sunday, he dragged her along with him, cutting a zigzag path toward a cluster of jagged boulders that leaned against each other like a natural tepee. A good defensive position, he decided, and a place where he could treat Maggie's wound.

"King, you're hurting me," she cried in a breathless voice.

"Don't worry, sweetheart. I'm going to take care of you." He couldn't figure out why with every step she seemed to be fighting him.

She stumbled, and his heart ripped apart the same painful way her flesh had been torn asunder with a bullet that should have been his. "You're going to be okay, Maggie girl. I swear it."

"If you don't let me go this instant, I'm going to strangle you."

Only concerned with Maggie's safety, King shoved her gently but unceremoniously into the protective niche he had spotted. Obviously she was already suffering from shock. With as much blood as she'd lost—it was oozing all over his hand—she was lucky to still be conscious.

With shaking hands he tried to unclasp the belt that held her backpack around her hips.

"What are you doing, you lunatic?" she objected in a hoarse whisper. "This is no time to try to get into my pants."

"You've been hit, honey. You're not feeling any pain right now but you will. I've got to stop the bleeding."

"You've got to stop pawing me, you bloody fool. I haven't been hit."

"Of course you have." He held out his hand to show her the dark, coagulating substance.

"Oh, my God," she cried on a soft intake of air. Her eyes widened in terror and her hand flew to her hip, the source of the hemorrhage.

She swiped her fingers along the back of her pants, then brought her hand close to her face to study the evidence of her wound. Frowning, she sniffed her palm.

"Don't panic, honey. Just let me get your backpack off and we'll see—"

"Ketchup." A high-pitched giggle enveloped the word.

"What?" King scowled. She was really losing it now. He'd heard of combat soldiers—

"The bullet got the plastic container in the backpack that's full of ketchup. That's what's running down my butt. I'm not hurt at all."

He exhaled and sank back on his haunches. "You're not?" He could have sworn . . .

"Well, don't sound so disappointed," she protested in a voice that was half offended and half on the edge of hysteria. "I could have been killed, you know."

"Yeah." And the danger was still out there somewhere even as darkness fell. A crazed treasure hunter with a rifle. *But who?* he wondered. The same guy who had shot Whitecloud? Or a second killer on the loose?

Knowing Maggie was all right, King returned his attention to the person or persons unknown who had taken a potshot at them. He strained to hear any movement beyond the boulders that sheltered them. He peered into the night that had fallen so quickly, leaving only a faint glow in the western sky.

In the deepest part of his gut he felt a wave of relief mixed with fear. Maggie wasn't out of danger yet. For that matter, neither was he.

"King," she whispered, "let's give them the map. No amount of gold is worth our lives."

"I'm not sure they'd be satisfied with only the map."

"Why on earth not?" Maggie shrugged off her pack and raised herself to a seated position with her back against the granite rock. "Surely they're just after the money."

"Maybe that's how it started. But now..."

She grabbed his upper arm, squeezing with more strength than King would have thought possible for someone so delicate, so slender, so totally feminine. "There's something you're not telling me, isn't there?" she asked grimly.

Confession time. King swallowed uncomfortably. "You remember my friend Whitecloud?" King could have used one of his buddy's magic Great Spirit visions about now.

"Of course. What about him?"

"He's dead. Whoever is out there—" he gestured toward the empty blackness "—is probably the guy who shot him."

"Shot?" Maggie's voice caught on the word.

"Afraid so. It happened at my Malibu place."

As King explained what had happened, Maggie let loose with a string of very unladylike expletives in several different languages, some of them Indian, he suspected. King barely suppressed a smile. This was one emotional lady when the cards were on the table. Or when she was in his bed, he mentally added.

"You brought me up here knowing...*knowing* that somebody wanted that map so badly they were ready to kill for it? Of all the nerve. How could you be so uncaring? I swear you'd risk your own grandmother's neck for a thrill."

"It wasn't quite like that, Maggie girl."

"Quit calling me Maggie!" she snapped, pushing him out of her way as she stood. "I'm getting out of here. If you want to keep the map, it's fine with me. But I don't want any part—"

Another shot slammed into the granite just above Maggie's head, exploding bits of rock into the air.

She screamed and ducked down again.

"Please, King, tell 'em we give up." Her voice trembled.

What choice did he have? He couldn't go on risking Maggie's life.

"We're coming out!" he shouted at the unknown assailant. "Don't shoot."

Silence greeted his attempted surrender. King didn't like the sound of that. If the shooter had been Smooth-Head Luke, the guy would have been gloating already. A stranger was far less predictable. And more dangerous.

"You hear me?" he shouted. "You can have the map but don't shoot. We're not armed." King unsheathed the hunting knife he now wore at his waist and balanced it in his palm. That was one little secret he didn't plan to reveal. Not that the weapon would do him much good against a rifle. At least, not at this range.

When there was still no response, King picked up a rock. Crouching near the entrance to their hideaway he tossed the stone about twenty feet down the hillside. Granite clinked against granite.

The shot that followed sent a shower of sparks in the air from the spot the two rocks had met.

"Damn," he muttered. The guy was one hell of a good marksman. The hole he'd drilled in White-cloud's forehead had been no fluke.

Maggie gasped. "They're not going to let us get out of here alive, are they?" she asked. Her hoarse voice betrayed her terror, and King cursed himself again.

"It's not looking good," he admitted.

"King, you've got to do something."

He did. He kissed her. Hard and hot and long enough so he could get his thoughts together, though the distraction of her sweet flavor made developing a strategy more of a challenge than he'd anticipated. By the time he heard her throaty sigh of surrender he knew there was only one plan that would work.

When he forced himself to pull away, his breath left his lungs in a ragged sigh. Before she could speak he covered her lips with his fingertip.

"You stay here," he whispered, his mouth against the intricate swirls of her ear.

"Where are you going?"

"There's a ledge about thirty, forty feet above us. I'm going to climb up there and make my way around behind that guy. I figure I can turn this ambush around."

"You can't leave me here alone."

"It's better this way, sweetheart. I'll get in position and then at first light I'll circle down and come up behind him. I'll have surprise on my side."

"What if he's not the patient sort and decides to come after us now? What am I supposed to do trapped in here all alone? Smile and invite him to tea?"

"I'd rather you didn't." King scowled. Spotting the attacker in the dark wouldn't be easy. Waiting till dawn would be a whole lot better, but Maggie had made a good point. She'd be far too vulnerable on her own.

"If you go, I go," she said with finality.

"It's too dangerous. You could fall and break your pretty little neck."

"So could you. The guy who is after us is definitely an equal-opportunity assassin. Our best chance is to outmaneuver him and do it now."

Before King could stop her Margaret slipped out of their hiding place. She scuttled along low to the ground, as she'd seen them do in old war movies, and tried to move as silently as possible. No way was King going to leave her all alone. If she was going to die, she wanted to be with him—preferably with him kissing her senseless.

He certainly knew how to do that to perfection. Her body still pulsated with his most recent humdinger. It was total madness that he would kiss her, that she most assuredly would kiss him back, when a killer was on the loose and they were the targets. Even now it didn't seem possible that she'd felt such fire leaping between them when the threat of a murderer only yards away should have cooled her ardor.

Maybe nothing would ever cure Margaret of her addiction to King. Pursing her kiss-swollen lips, she decided that even the grave might not make a difference.

As Margaret reached a wall of rock, King clamped a hand on her shoulder. He signaled that he was going to lead the way up to the ledge. That was just fine with Margaret. She hated heights anyway. At least she'd silenced his objections to her coming along.

Cracks and crannies cut the granite face as if some inept giant had been carelessly creating a castle with crooked building blocks. Each fissure offered a welcome toehold or handhold, making climbing difficult but not impossible. Margaret labored upward in King's wake. Her heavy breathing and rapid heartbeat thundered in her ears, the harmonics of her body an anvil chorus she was sure could be heard all the way to Tuolumne Meadows. Her muscles strained against gravity and fatigue.

She froze in place when King loosened a shower of noisy pebbles down on her. Splayed against the rock wall as they were, Margaret could only pray there wasn't enough starlight for the guy with the rifle to see their shadows on the granite.

Above her, King stayed as immobile as she.

They waited for long, breathless moments. Waited for a bullet to tear through their bodies. Waited for a handhold to give way and send them crashing back down to earth. Margaret waited and wondered what King was thinking about.

Surely she wouldn't react so strongly every time he touched her if he weren't feeling something, too.

She really should have read more of those self-help books. Like how to communicate with a man. Or, more to the point, how to avoid falling in love with the *wrong* guy.

With a mental effort she tried to place her thoughts into some kind of rational order, like classifying artifacts. King did care about her. She'd heard the concern, the real fear in his voice when he'd believed she'd been shot. Of course, she thought with a silent sigh, he could just as easily have been experiencing a load of guilt.

But intuitively she believed there was more to King's feelings for her than that. On the other hand, maybe that was simply wishful thinking.

After what seemed an eternity, King cautiously resumed the ascent. Margaret's tremulous muscles rebelled as she renewed her efforts.

A few minutes later King wrapped his hand around her wrist and lifted her easily over the edge onto a treacherously narrow ledge. She lay beneath him, her arms wrapped around his middle, and wished they were anywhere else in the world. But together. Always together. A fantasy that wasn't likely to come true.

"You okay?" he asked.

Breathless, she nodded against his shoulder.

"Whenever you're ready, let me know."

Margaret was *ready* to settle down in a split-level house with a double garage and two-point-seven normal, average kids. At this particular moment even the idea of carpooling to soccer games and hauling the kids to piano lessons had considerable appeal. She definitely wasn't ready for murderers and wolverine attacks, or the persistent and totally tantalizing notion that no day would ever be boring if she was with King.

Her fingers flexed in frustration and she was filled with regret that she could only grasp the thickness of his jacket instead of the sensuous feel of his flesh.

King felt her shift beneath his body. He stifled a groan. This was no time to be thinking how he'd like to sheath himself within Maggie's warmth. Their position was downright perilous, both in terms of the narrow ledge and the guy who was waiting in ambush for them. One false move on their part and it would be curtains for them both.

Not a happy thought.

Yet the reluctance he felt about releasing Maggie from his hold was a palpable thing, a creation of smoldering coals and dark nights spent among lonely memories. He'd walked away from her once and he knew he'd have to do it again. The curse he carried was too heavy a burden to place on the delicate shape of Maggie's shoulders.

With a resigned sigh Margaret whispered, "Lead on, McDermott." She imagined she'd follow him to the ends of the earth, if he'd let her, then castigated herself for the thought. That kind of thinking would buy her nothing but trouble.

On hands and knees they edged along the mountain's shoulder, a ledge better suited to a mountain goat than to human travelers in slow encirclement of an assassin. A sudden wind had kicked up, lifting loose snow into powdery clouds that drifted down the cliff in a protective curtain. Somewhere beyond the mist a hunter with a high-powered rifle waited. For them.

Margaret kept her terror at bay by following closely behind King. Vaguely she wondered if she had become a lemming bent on going over a cliff in thoughtless pursuit of her leader.

After an interminable time the ledge funneled into a natural—though shallow—cave that provided both shelter and a break from the wind. In spite of the cold air, the partial enclosure smelled of rock, dust and animal leavings.

"This is far enough," King said, pulling her up close to his body for warmth. "I think we're behind him now."

Margaret concentrated on recovering her breath and her mental equilibrium.

"King," she said after a few minutes' respite, "what are we going to do when we spot the guy in the morning?"

When he didn't answer right away she felt a new wave of anxiety.

Speaking so softly her voice wouldn't carry beyond King's hearing, she said, "I don't want to be a part of killing anyone. I don't think I could do it."

"Whatever has to be done, I'll take care of it, sweetheart."

"Have you...? I mean, in the past, did you ever...?" In so many ways she knew very little about King. They had more often communicated on a visceral rather than intellectual level, and that they had done exceptionally well, to her way of thinking.

"If you're asking if I've ever killed anyone, the answer is not that I know of. I'm kind of a pacifist at heart."

"Me, too." Reassured, she smiled and rested her head on his shoulder. "Then what are we going to do?"

He chuckled, a low, rumbling sound that should have been totally inappropriate given the circumstances. Instead it was warm and comforting, a bit like whistling in a graveyard, Margaret imagined, though the thought of a cemetery gave her a sudden case of the shivers.

King hugged her a little tighter. "If we were Maori warriors, we could dance around, slap our stomachs, grunt and holler and make ugly faces to scare the guy off. How are you at sticking out your tongue?"

"Not funny, King." She felt the lulling brush of his lips on her forehead. "Tell me this. How did someone catch up with us so fast? It's not like we took the scenic route." Except for a few rest stops, and their scramble over the avalanche, they'd made steady progress all day.

"Whoever is out there is probably traveling alone, and we very thoughtfully packed the trail for him. All he had to do was stay right in our tracks. He could make a lot better time than we could."

"So instead of an avalanche, that *was* another snowmobile I heard this morning," she said with quick realization.

"Very possibly. Unless the guy has wings."

King rested his cheek against Maggie's head, catching the scent of her herbal shampoo. He didn't know quite what he was going to do in the morning. Somehow he'd have to sneak up on the killer. Not an easy assignment. Then, at the very least, he'd have to disarm the guy.

The one thing he was absolutely sure about was that no way was the fellow going to get hold of Maggie.

With a determined straightening of his spine, King adjusted his position and his hand balled into a fist. Whatever it took.

"You're planning to do something foolish tomorrow, aren't you?" she asked, as though she'd just read his mind.

"I got us into this mess. I'll get us out."

Turning her head, she looked up at him and placed her gloved hand on his cheek. "Whatever happens, we're going to do it together. So don't try going heroic on me."

He didn't want to be anyone's hero. Certainly not a dead one.

What he wanted was to make love to Maggie all night and forget about the morning. Unfortunately, the narrow burrow they'd found didn't allow much moving around, much less stretching out to a comfortable position. He could only imagine lying beside her, caressing the swell of her breasts and suckling at her nipples. He might want to taste the intimate nectar of her womanhood but he damned well couldn't do that now.

Yet the memory of how she felt in his arms, her soft cries of passion and surrender, was as fresh in his mind as a bite of ripe fruit plucked from a tree. And his hunger was a gnawing, urgent thing impossible to control. Any thought of risk, from his feelings for

Maggie, or from some guy with a rifle, fled from his mind.

He captured her hand, the sigh of her name a raspy sound deep in his throat. Adrenaline surged through his veins. God, he wanted this woman as he'd never wanted any other.

The fire flared as soon as he tasted the sweet velvet of her mouth. He savored the heat. He stroked his tongue against her soft ridges and valleys that had lain hidden from him too long. Deeper and deeper he penetrated. With only a low moan, which could have been a yes or a no, she accepted his explorations.

She wrapped her arms around his shoulders, tugging him closer in tempting encouragement. He needed little more urging.

His hands slid over her in search of her familiar landscape—the curve of her spine, the flare of her hip, her firm, rounded thighs and the sheltered crevice between them.

She gasped when he touched her there.

With a jagged breath Margaret pulled her lips away, and his mouth sought the tender skin below her ear for a new erotic exploration, while his fingers continued a circling invasion of her lower body. His seductive onslaught intensified until it became a flame, licking at her reason, sucking the air from her lungs. A euphoria of passion weighted her limbs. She struggled against the dragging pull, the sudden absence of oxygen that made her light-headed, only to find in each movement a torturous renewal of desire.

"We can't do this," she protested even as she trembled in his arms. "Not here. Not now."

"I know." He'd stop in a minute, King promised himself. Yet as she writhed against his hand he knew he would never stop until at least one of them had found some relief from the insistent heat that burned within them both.

With his other hand he speared his fingers through her hair and dragged her mouth up to meet his again. With long, lingering strokes of his tongue he tormented her, and did the same with the heel of his hand between her thighs. Even as she tried to renew her protest, her body arched against him. Her need for physical connection was as urgent as his own.

In every way he could within the limited confines of the cave, he pleasured Maggie. Her scent and heat filled the air. Without a word he praised her uninhibited responses and encouraged her with more caresses that penetrated bulky clothing as though it was sheer silk.

With a groan of frustration he imagined how her unfettered breasts would feel in his palms, her rigid nipples taste on his lips. Sweet, hot velvet, inaccessible for now but vivid in his mind.

His body burned with need. If only he could sheathe himself in her tight entrance, the ache would be eased, but that wasn't possible. Damn lousy timing.

With his hand he increased the pressure and Maggie's pleasure until he felt her buck violently against him. He deepened the kiss as her muffled cry of release filled his throat.

"That's my girl...."

Chapter Seven

"That wasn't fair." Margaret drew a shuddering breath and collapsed against King, limp and exhausted.

"Don't tell me you didn't enjoy every minute," he mocked, his voice low and husky and as breathless as her own.

"What did you expect me to do? Scream and go running out of here, right into the arms of some killer?" Admittedly, in many ways that would have been a much safer course. "You took advantage," she accused.

"Yeah, I did," he drawled. "Aren't you glad?"

No. Furious was closer to the mark. Furious with herself because she couldn't have stopped King's caresses and his soul-deep kisses if her life had depended upon it.

And she hated him for making her acknowledge the truth, even if it was only to herself. He knew her weaknesses and played on them with the same skill a pagan priest used to mesmerize a willing victim into the ultimate self-sacrifice. She had given herself up to him, given in to the primitive urges he had long ago discovered, and she hated him for finding them again so easily. She had thought she'd buried them so deeply they'd never trouble her again. She'd been wrong. Oh, so very wrong.

But something else had happened, too. In a way she hadn't imagined, she'd discovered she had a power over King that was almost...*almost* as overwhelming as his effect on her. No matter what he'd said, he wasn't above the fray.

Damn it all! He cared. It was more than sex. She knew that with the same ferocity as a wolverine on the attack.

As she settled weakly into his arms and buried her face against his broad chest, Margaret decided she'd simply have to show him. If it was the last thing on earth she'd ever do, she'd make King admit he cared about her.

Then, by God, she'd walk away, just as he'd left her in Santa Fe. No way would she be the one to set a trap for him. She had more pride than that.

With another silent curse she swiped the back of her hand against the press of tears. Somehow she'd show him....

STEALTH.

King slipped and slid silently down the hill with all the caution he'd learned from his many nefarious adventures. Blowing snow peppered his face; Maggie's hand clung to his jacket. She was right on his tail, practically walking in his footprints.

This wasn't going to work, he realized.

"Maggie, sweetheart, you can't stay so close to me," he whispered.

"Why not? We're doing this together, remember?"

"It's not good strategy, that's why. We've got a lot better chance of catching the guy off guard if we approach him from two different directions." There would also be far less chance of Maggie getting hurt if she was well away from King.

"But I want to stay close to you," she pleaded.

"I may need you to distract him. If you're right on top of me, it's too likely he will have us both in his sights."

She studied him with a skeptical eye. "Are you sure you're not trying to get rid of me?"

"Not a chance, sweetheart." He pointed off to the right. "You slip down that gully over there. You'll have good cover and if I've misjudged where the guy is . . . well, you'll be able to help me out."

For a moment she contemplated his proposal. Then, with obvious reluctance, she nodded her agreement.

King blew out a sigh as she moved away—out of danger, he hoped. He resumed his descent, keeping his body as low to the terrain as he could manage, barely able to see Maggie's crouched shadow moving just as slowly through the mist a dozen paces off to his right.

Strangely, above him the dawning sky shone a silver-blue.

If the low-blowing blizzard protected King from being spotted by the killer, it also hid the guy in the same eerie phenomenon. King had to work on instinct alone. He'd calculated exactly where he would have waited in ambush if the situation had been reversed. It was a little like a billiard problem, he decided, contemplating possible angles and carom shots. Of course, the stakes were a whole hell of a lot higher.

He weaseled his way around a particularly large outcropping of rock, losing sight of Maggie for a moment, and then arrowed back to his original track. The guy was good. There hadn't been a single sound all night that gave away his location. A simple cough would have been a helpful clue.

It was possible the killer had given it up as a bad idea and stolen off under the cover of darkness.

But the raised hackles on the back of King's neck told him that wasn't the case. Somebody was down there. Waiting.

Even moving cautiously, King found the footing treacherous, a layered combination of snow and ice. His boots weren't exactly made for hiking. He worried that Maggie might be having trouble, too. If either of them made a false step and started a snowfall, the killer would be sure to hear them. Surprise was their only real ally.

King stayed above the trail they'd followed the previous day. He wanted the advantage of height. On the far side of the winding route he knew the drop was nearly vertical. He wasn't anxious to find himself on the down side of some guy with a rifle. Or at the bottom of the ravine with his neck broken.

He picked up a handful of snow to moisten his dry mouth. His heart beat low, heavy strokes against his ribs. Maybe he was getting too old for treasure hunting. Too bad there wasn't a place to apply for retirement benefits right about now.

Pausing, King took a deep breath. He was going to have to risk exposure if he was to have any chance of spotting the guy.

Standing slowly, King raised his head above the shifting mist, his gaze darting back and forth along the trail.

From somewhere off in the distance King had the distinct impression he heard Indian beads rattle. Ridiculous. But at that very moment the wind stopped and the snow settled softly back to the ground, as if there'd never been any wind blowing at all. Then King saw the killer standing right below him.

Way to go, Whitecloud! Having an Indian mystic on your side was a definite plus even if King didn't quite understand what was going on. He should have listened more carefully to the old man's crazy stories of spirits returning from the dead. But this wasn't the time to dwell on unanswered questions.

Knife in hand, King leaped at the parka-clad figure.

Some barely heard noise alerted the killer.

Whirling, with the rifle shifting from its target of the tepeed rocks to King's hurtling body, the killer cried out a startled sound.

The alpine air exploded with a single rifle shot.

Too late King realized the killer was a woman. Before he crashed into her he had a fleeting impression of dark hair and almond-shaped eyes. He barely managed to avert burying his knife up to its hilt in her belly.

The force of his impact, the shoulder he'd lowered, sent her stumbling backward. Wide-eyed, she stared

at him for a heart-stopping moment, her arms flailing
the air for balance, the rifle slipping from her grasp,
and then she teetered back over the precipice. Her
scream echoed, ricocheting with a pathetic ring along
the steep canyon sides.

King fell to his knees. He gulped for breath. "Son
of a gun...."

MARGARET LABORED THROUGH knee-deep snow to
reach King. Dear God, he'd been shot. The pain she
felt was so intense it was as though the bullet had
ripped through her own flesh. Her heart seemed to
split apart at an unseen seam.

"King..." His name tore at her throat as she
dropped beside him.

"The Tuolumne ranger," he replied with a hoarse-
ness that grated along Margaret's spine even as she
celebrated that he was still alive and apparently un-
harmed. "Who would have guessed..."

"But why?" she cried, nausea threatening when
King confirmed the glimpse she'd gotten of the young
woman just before she fell. Granted, Margaret had
been jealous of the ranger, even suspected her of
stealing from the skiers. But attempted murder? "Why
would she try to kill us?"

"We won't know until I go down there and check it
out. There's got to be something on her that will give
us a clue about what's going on."

Her hand gripping his arm restrained him for the
moment. "It's too dangerous, King. You could fall. It
must be a hundred-foot drop."

He covered her hand with his, squeezing gently. In response, her heart constricted painfully. She knew there would be no stopping him. Just her luck to tumble for a guy who was always trying to be so damn heroic. As easygoing as he might appear, he was too damn stubborn for his own good. Or hers.

"I'll find an easy way down." He palmed her face, his gaze surveying her pale cheeks and the slight tremor of her chin. "Thanks for caring."

"I assure you, my interest is purely selfish," she blustered. "If you fall and break your leg, where would that leave me?"

He arched a well-shaped brow, a spark of amusement in his eyes. "You'd have the treasure all to yourself," he pointed out.

"Don't count on it. The way things have been going, my guess is there could be another dozen or so bad guys out there just waiting to pounce on us."

"An unpleasant possibility," he conceded, "and all the more reason why I have to check out Diane."

She questioned him with a frown.

"Maybe there's something on her that will give us an idea of who she's working for, or if she's a solo act," he explained. "If she has a partner, then we're going to have to keep watching our backs."

Margaret didn't like the sound of that. She also wasn't pleased with the idea of King searching the dead woman's pockets, or whatever he'd have to do. The ghoulish thought sent a shudder down her back.

"Why don't we go back to Tuolumne and let the park service take care of all this?" she asked without having much hope King would accept her plan.

Granted, she wanted her share of the treasure for the museum, but the price tag seemed to be rising by the minute.

"Because, my innocent little miss, if there is a partner, he'd be waiting there for Diane's return. If he spotted us..." King ran the back of his gloved hand along Margaret's cheek. "Well, I'd rather not think about what might happen then."

She didn't want to imagine that kind of confrontation, either. Particularly if the partner was someone the size of Crazy Arnold. Or had his own bowie knife, like Little John. Margaret's throat still sported a scab where that hoodlum had pricked her. It was, she recalled with a race of heat to her face, one of those ultrasensitive spots on her neck where King had kissed her during the night.

Lord, no other man in the world knew her pleasure zones with such precision, knew so instinctively how to arouse her. She appeared quite helpless to prevent all the delicious feelings he effortlessly created. With characteristic honesty she admitted she hadn't made much of an effort to stop his determined and thoroughly erotic attack on her senses last night. And she wouldn't the next time, either, she acknowledged with a mix of regret and anticipation.

Beyond all reason, she wanted his sweet, melting fire. No matter that he led her down a path that risked both her life and her heart. She wanted King.

And he was the one man in all the world whom she shouldn't desire. He had the power to give her more pain than any woman should be asked to endure...

even if in the end she had the bittersweet courage to be the one to leave this time around.

"Go if you must," she ordered with a lift of her chin. "But if you break your fool neck, I'll never speak to you again."

KING CHOSE A CIRCUITOUS route to the bottom of the canyon rather than attempting the vertical drop where Diane had fallen to her death. A brief search of her body left more troubling questions than answers. He marked the spot with a red bandanna tied to a twisted pine, so someone would be able to recover the body later. Then he made his way back to Maggie.

"Your guess was right about the diary," King said, handing her the leather-bound book he'd found tucked inside the would-be ranger's parka.

Margaret accepted the journal with a grateful sigh. At least the museum hadn't permanently lost an irreplaceable archive... assuming she lived long enough to return the book to its rightful place. "Why would a ranger—"

"She was no more a park service employee than I am. Her ID says she comes from Vegas and goes by the name of Tempest Storm. A show girl, would be my guess." He squinted up at the bright sky, a troubled frown creasing his forehead with two wavy lines. "Smooth-Head owns an interest in a casino in Vegas."

"Then the two of them are connected in some way?"

"Possibly. She also had a copy of Whitecloud's map. I suspect she'd gotten as far as Tuolumne and then waited around for *somebody* to show up who knew where they were going. It turned out to be us. The diary was an added attraction she hadn't expected. No question, if we hadn't gotten out of there in a hurry, we never would have made it out alive."

Instead, a beautiful, though misguided, young woman had died a tragic death for a few bags of gold, Margaret thought, idly turning the pages of the diary.

"Do you think she's the one who killed your friend?" she asked.

"It's possible. She was a damn good shot."

"But if she already had the map, why would she resort to murder?"

"Eliminating the competition, I imagine."

Margaret blew out another long sigh. She definitely wasn't used to this kind of stress. "We could populate a small town with the number of people who are after those gold coins," she said. "They either have, or know about, that darn map. As far as I can tell, your fellow treasure hunters aren't very nice people."

"Greed makes for dangerous bedfellows."

"Then why don't we just throw in the towel, King? You don't need the money and...well, the museum will survive some way." Though at the moment, she didn't quite see how. She was simply trying to establish priorities. At the moment, breathing on a regular basis seemed to be at the top of the list.

"Wish it was that easy, sweetheart." He looped an arm casually around her shoulders and she felt a sweet ache tighten her throat. "Truth is, we aren't going to be safe until we find the gold and get it stashed in some very solid vault, preferably the U.S. Mint.''

''You're serious, aren't you?''

He slanted her a look that knotted her stomach with fear. ''Very. I don't know where Diane, or rather Tempest, got her information, and it really doesn't matter. Where there's one map, there could be dozens more. And any number of them could have fallen into the wrong hands.''

''King, I'm scared.''

''We'll be okay.'' His voice carried a lot of confidence that she suspected was forced.

He led her back to where they had left their gear the previous evening. When they reached the snowmobile he started to check out the vehicle while she went to retrieve her backpack. What she found sent her heart plummeting.

''King!'' she cried, sickened by the way the contents of her pack were strewn all around the rock shelter where they'd briefly hidden the night before.

Responding to her urgent call, King joined her, coming to an abrupt halt. ''What the devil happened?''

''From the footprints, it looks like the wolverine came to call again. Look at this.'' She held up the shredded pack. ''My guess is that ketchup is a wolverine delicacy. He started at that corner of the pack and worked his way through all the food packets to the main course.''

Muttering a curse, King knelt beside her. ''Not much food left, is there?'' He sorted through the mess. A single package of freeze-dried Stroganoff and a

NO RISK, NO OBLIGATION TO BUY...NOW OR EVER!

GUARANTEED

PLAY "ROLL A DOUBLE" AND GET AS MANY AS FIVE FREE GIFTS!

HERE'S HOW TO PLAY:

1. Peel off label from front cover. Place it in space provided at right. With a coin, carefully scratch off the silver dice. This makes you eligible to receive two or more free books, and possibly another gift, depending on what is revealed beneath the scratch-off area.

2. Send back this card and you'll receive brand-new Harlequin American Romance® novels. These books have a cover price of $3.50 each, but they are yours to keep absolutely free.

3. There's no catch. You're under no obligation to buy anything. We charge nothing – ZERO – for your first shipment. And you don't have to make any minimum number of purchases – not even one!

4. The fact is thousands of readers enjoy receiving books by mail from the Harlequin Reader Service® months before they're available in stores. They like the convenience of home delivery and they love our discount prices!

5. We hope that after receiving your free books you'll want to remain a subscriber. But the choice is yours – to continue or cancel, anytime at all! So why not take us up on our invitation, with no risk of any kind. You'll be glad you did!

THE HARLEQUIN READER SERVICE®: HERE'S HOW IT WORKS

Accepting free books puts you under no obligation to buy anything. You may keep the books and gift and return the shipping statement marked "cancel." If you do not cancel, about a month later we will send you 4 additional novels, and bill you just $2.71 each plus 25¢ delivery and applicable sales tax, if any.* That's the complete price, and – compared to cover prices of $3.50 each – quite a bargain! You may cancel at any time, but if you choose to continue, every month we'll send you 4 more books, which you may either purchase at the discount price...or return at our expense and cancel your subscription.

*Terms and prices subject to change without notice. Sales tax applicable in N.Y.

smashed box of pancake mix remained in their larder. Slim pickings for the remainder of the trip. There was nothing left but the tent and other nonedible gear stuffed in the saddlebags on the snowmobile.

"We're going to have to give it up after all, King."

He contemplated her suggestion until she thought he surely would agree. Then that familiar mischievous twinkle appeared in his eyes. With a sinking feeling in the pit of her stomach Margaret knew she was still in trouble.

"No problem," he announced, busily stuffing what he could of their equipment back into the pack and tying it closed with the straps. "We'll live off the land."

"In the middle of winter? You're crazy."

"The Sherpas in Nepal used to—"

"King, there's at least six feet of snow on the ground, and that's in sheltered spots. As near as I can tell, there aren't any Sherpas running around here. We can't possibly—"

"I'll make some snares and we'll have roasted rabbit for dinner. How does that sound?"

He'd announced the menu with such confidence Margaret could almost believe he was a chef in a five-star restaurant. Almost... but not quite.

"Just how many times have you actually caught a rabbit in a snare?" she asked, suspicion tugging her eyebrows down.

He shrugged. "It can't be that hard."

"Have you ever seen it done?"

"Where's your sense of adventure?"

"I don't like adventure," she protested with a groan. "I like my days carefully planned. I like to know where I'll sleep every night...and what I'm having for dinner. In fact, I make it a point to plan my menus a whole week in advance." She planted one fist on the curve of her hip. "Rabbit isn't included on the list this week."

"Ah, Maggie girl, now I see the problem." He gave her a lopsided grin and the corners of his eyes crinkled with amusement. "Don't you know the sun will come up every morning whether you plan for it or not? The fun in living is to enjoy the unexpected. It's the *not* knowing where you'll be when the sun goes down that adds spice to life."

She fought a traitorous temptation to go along with his wild scheme. "We'll starve," she warned.

His silver-blue eyes warmed to indigo and he held her gaze for several heart-stopping beats. She read his mind as easily as a billboard—*there are more powerful hungers than food alone can satisfy.* Or maybe those were her own thoughts she heard.

She licked her winter-chapped lips and his gaze followed the quick dart of her tongue. In spite of the cool air, a liquid heat curled through her belly and settled heavily between her thighs. The throbbing sensation muted the intelligent voice that urged prudence on a foolish woman.

"Maybe I can find some edible roots or bulbs under the snow to supplement our diet," she suggested, admitting defeat. She'd studied Indian lore most of her life, including their eating habits. She was an expert, she reminded herself. Surely she could use that knowledge to fill their empty stomachs.

His victorious grin sent a new surge of longing to Margaret's heart. "That's my girl," he said in a low, intimate tone.

She silently acknowledged that there was only one place she wanted to be tonight—in King's arms. If she had to go on a forced diet, it would be worth the price.

"Here, let me do that for you," she said, taking the pack from King and dumping the contents out again. In the side pocket she found the small sewing kit she'd brought along. "I'd just as soon not have our little remaining gear falling out along the trail. I should be able to sew up this hole enough to hold it together for a couple of days." And that was about all the time she'd have with King. Then he'd be off on some new adventure while she returned to the quiet life of a museum curator. Maybe in another four or five years he'd drop by again, rather as her father had appeared, to have dinner with his family, on rare occasions.

Margaret could still remember how excited she'd been to have all three members of her family together, her father telling wonderful tales of his latest invention. Or how the backers he'd hoped to convince of its merits had once again been shortsighted. Within hours he would have vanished into his own special world again, to a place where Margaret couldn't follow, even though it was only a dilapidated garage behind the house.

At the ripe old age of ten she'd vowed that when she had a family they'd always be together.

Not much chance of that happening with a man like King, she acknowledged with a painful sense of regret.

King sat back on his haunches watching Maggie thread a needle. She studied the tear in the backpack, a cute little frown furrowing her forehead. The tip of her tongue appeared as she took the first stitch and then another, carefully linking the jagged edges together.

A very domestic lady.

He couldn't remember his own mother sewing a stitch. The wife of a prominent newspaper publisher didn't have to do that sort of thing. She had servants, all dutifully checked out by the police as being harmless, who took care of mundane tasks. Or if a button popped off a dress, she simply bought a new one.

King wondered if Maggie would even like that kind of life, and somehow imagined not. She was a very independent lady. Having to be chauffeured to the museum every day by a guy who toted a gun would cramp her freedom and make her a miserable old crone before her time—just like his mother.

Still, Maggie did have the most fascinating tongue, he conceded, observing the way she unconsciously licked her lips. Soft velvet with the sweet taste of ambrosia.

He stared at her profile, her upturned nose, the curve of her lips and that tempting tongue. For just a moment his heart went all soft and wanting, while another part of his anatomy had the opposite reaction. He fought the former sensation and ignored, for now, the latter. There'd be time enough tonight to get her into his sleeping bag. An interlude. That was all he wanted. That was all he dared hope for.

In some strange way he'd always felt that was all he deserved. As his parents had reminded him rather frequently, his brother had had far less.

WHEN MARGARET MOUNTED the snowmobile, her pack was whole again, much lighter than it had been before, and the sun was high in the sky. Yesterday the snow had been firm and smooth along the trail. Now it was wet, almost heavy, with the sun beating down on the white expanse.

They were barely under way when it happened—a crack like the report of a distant cannon.

Margaret snapped her head around to look back the way they had come. Huge sheets of ice and frozen snow crashed off the mountainside. Great chunks became airborne, tossing and turning in acrobatic dives, triggering secondary slides of snow and rock that careered downward, altering the terrain and burying the trail under tons of debris. The monumental sound shattered the stillness and reverberated in Margaret's head, along with a growing sense of panic.

Now there could be no turning back.

With new understanding, Margaret glanced directly above them. In the glistening sun she recognized the dangerous layers of ice interspersed with snow.

Her heart lodged in her throat.

The canyon was a death trap.

King understood the danger, too. Bracing himself, he accelerated the snowmobile to full throttle. He felt the frightened tug of Maggie's arms around his waist, and he chided himself once again for putting her in harm's way. This was a race that he could understand. The specter of death had always hovered on his shoulder. He'd grown immune, challenging the ever-threatening presence to "get me if you can." In a way, he'd thrived by thumbing his nose at both natural and man-made perils. That was how he'd survived.

But he knew it wasn't Maggie's kind of game.

Above the sound of the snowmobile he heard another thunderous roar. Slivers of ice and snow showered down around them. King drove with a new urgency to reach the valley beyond the unending canyon walls.

The vehicle toiled in the wet snow, unable to rise above the dragging weight. King felt as though they were moving in slow motion. Only his heart responded to the danger with a painful surge of acceleration.

Ahead of him King spotted a swath already cut across the trail by the awesome power of an avalanche, the snows now quiet and at rest. If he could just make it that far, they'd be safe, at least for the moment. Straining with every fiber in his body, he concentrated on getting Maggie to that single island of safety.

Too late.

The thunder of collapsing snow roared right above them.

King glanced up to see a puff of white, innocent for the moment, and then it took on shape and form and mass, barreling unchecked down the precipice, gain-ing momentum with every foot it fell. Snow and ice answered the irrefutable demands of gravity with a frightening roar.

With only seconds to act, King launched the snow-mobile over the lip of the canyon, a small barrier that might afford some modicum of protection. He shouted, "Hang on!"

The machine caught the edge at an awkward angle and the vehicle hurtled into the air, separating itself from the riders. Earth and sky tumbled in blue-and-white confusion. Maggie's scream penetrated the roar of what sounded like a fast-approaching freight train.

King felt her grasp around his belly slip. Frantically he grabbed her, wrapping his fingers around her slender wrist, and held on tight as the howling assault battered his senses. There seemed to be no up or down. Cold, white chaos, punctuated by rocks slamming into his back and shoulders, dazed and disoriented King. The only thing that was real, the only thought that mattered, was the feel of Maggie's weight tugging on his arm.

And then it was over, almost as soon as the wild ride down the slope had started.

King's ears still rang even though silence had returned to the mountain. He felt light-headed. His body ached from a dozen bruises that he'd worry about later. Right now he had to figure out which way was up. Then he'd see to Maggie.

Dear God, her wrist felt limp and lifeless in his hand.

His first gulp of fresh air burned his lungs. He drew in another painful breath and began to dig through the

snow. Though she hadn't been buried deeply or for
many minutes, Maggie showed no response when he
uncovered her face. Melted snow starred her silver
lashes. Except for the stigmata of cold, her cheeks
were deathly pale. With a tenderness that was both
painful and filled with remorse, King felt for her pulse.

Her lashes fluttered.

King blew out a sigh. "Come on, Maggie girl. This
is no time to take a nap."

Margaret tried to snuggle deeper into the cocoon
that held her so tightly. But it was cold. Really cold.
And a familiar masculine voice wouldn't let her sleep.
She couldn't quite make out what he was saying, but
she didn't think it made much difference, because
she'd never be able to understand his words over the
incredibly loud pounding that was going on in her
head. She did her best to ignore the words as well as
the anvil chorus that had moved in without her per-
mission.

The insistent voice wouldn't give up even when she
tried to slip back into cold oblivion. So she tried to
open her eyes, to tell the man to get lost, only to find
that everything was a blur. Her stomach did a quick
somersault and she groaned.

"That's my girl," the voice said with an amazing
amount of tenderness.

Margaret tried to concentrate. In spite of herself she
found she liked that voice—sort of deep and raspy and
thoroughly seductive. It made her think of cold nights
around a fire, warm, fuzzy slippers and strong arms
holding her. Rather pleasant thoughts, considering the
sharp pain radiating from the back of her skull.

The hands that belonged to the voice began to do intimate things to her. They lifted her leg, stroking along her calf, squeezing her knee, then drifted upward along her thigh. She really shouldn't allow herself to be taken advantage of like that. But then, she was enjoying the feel of his strong fingers exploring every inch of her anatomy and didn't exactly want him to stop.

When his hands reached her rib cage, moving inexorably upward, Margaret's eyes flew open. Heat suffused her, instantly melting the icy cold.

"King?" she cried, her senses back in focus, her body a good many degrees warmer than it had been only moments ago.

"Ah, you've decided to rejoin the living." A relieved smile tilted his lips.

Memory returned in a painful wince. "You blew it again, McDermott."

Frowning, he finger-combed the drooping hair that had fallen across her forehead. She got a shivery feeling that had nothing to do with snow.

"How many times is it," she asked, "that you've tried to be the death of me? I certainly don't go easily, do I?"

"That must be why I keep trying," he said wryly, his fingers trembling against her forehead.

The man would have failed a lie-detector test in the first twenty seconds. When push came to shove, he couldn't hide his feelings any more than Margaret could bury her own emotions when it came to King. Damn him all the way to Timbuktu! Not that it would do her any good.

Chapter Eight

"But I want to take a nap." Relaxed, and more weary than she would have thought possible, Margaret leaned back against the rough bark of the tree where she was sitting. The sleeping bag spread beneath her provided a soft mattress on top of the patch of snow. Pine branches sheltered her. She felt safe—safe from a sniper's attack, safe from the ravages of a runaway avalanche and men like Smooth-Head Luke.

"You can't sleep, Maggie girl. Not yet. In spite of your helmet you got a nasty bump on your head during the avalanche. Probably a concussion."

"I've had a long day. I'm tired." Every day since King had come back into her life had been long and wearing. Adventurous, too, Margaret admitted with a silent groan, and not in the least protected from a broken heart.

"The sun is just barely down," he pointed out. "It isn't time for bed yet. Besides, I have to keep checking your eyes."

"Your constant vigilance is admirable," she said with a fair amount of sarcasm. "But nothing's changed in the last fifteen minutes. I feel fine." Except for the dull headache that continued to nag her, and the warmed-honey feeling she got right between her thighs every time King looked so deeply into her eyes.

He lifted her chin to gaze at her again. The campfire he'd built in front of their ragged tent cast golden shadows across his face, accenting his handsome features and highlighting his evening stubble of whiskers. He'd managed to carry her beyond the threat of avalanches into a wide meadow, where he'd set her among a clump of hemlock and silver pines. She'd suffered the humiliation of being carried fireman-style because he simply wouldn't put her down, though he'd sunk to his knees under her weight more than once.

Then he'd gone back into the dangerous canyon again to retrieve what he could of their equipment. From the wrecked snowmobile he salvaged their tent and sleeping bags but little else.

Thinking of his strength and unfailing determination, she smiled up at him. Unable to resist, she touched his cheek, the sensitive nerves at the tips of her fingers relishing the roughened texture of his day-old beard. Slowly she drew a trail along the curve of his strong jaw. In the firelight she caught the glint of desire in his silver-blue eyes and felt a matching response deep within her body.

"I'm fine," she repeated in a whisper.

"You're right about hanging around with a guy like me," he said, his voice rough with a caring she knew he'd never admit. "It's too dangerous."

"I think I'm getting used to it. Or maybe I'm just numb." More likely the blow to her head had unbalanced her mentally. That was the only possible explanation for her not wanting to be anywhere except right here with King.

He sat down and she adjusted her position so they could share the same tree for a backrest. Their shoulders brushed together. The rich smell of cooked rabbit still lingered in the alpine air along with the scent of wood smoke. Contentedly full from the feast of spitted hare à la King, Margaret sighed. Camping had never been so good.

The fire crackled in a warm, cozy way; sparks drifted up toward the darkening sky. *If only time would stand still,* she thought, far too practical to indulge in such wishful thinking for very long. Yet the idea was tempting. Something about being around King invited a headful of romantic notions. *Dangerous notions,* she mentally corrected. Thoughts like *permanence* and *forever after* kept skittering through her mind. She didn't dare count on fantasies like that.

Mesmerized by the warmth and hypnotic flickering of the fire, she felt her eyelids growing heavy, her body languorous, as though waiting for the next step on a journey she'd begun a long time ago.

"I can see there's only one way I'm going to be able to keep you awake." King's low voice was a whispered intimacy close to her ear, his breath warm and inviting.

"What's that?" she asked as though she were unaware of his intentions. Sweet anticipation curled through her limbs. Since he'd carried her to safety she'd known they'd make love tonight. The shared aphrodisiac of danger had made it inevitable. Life was too precious to waste one single moment. Tomorrow, and the heartache that would very likely follow, would simply have to take care of themselves.

With his fingers he threaded her long hair back behind her ear, baring the sensitive shell for his inspection. When his moist tongue swept the swirls, a shiver arrowed down her spine. The flames of the campfire deepened to a darker red and licked at the wood, heating the pine branches in the same way that King brought an irresistible warmth to Margaret's heart. She drew an unsteady breath that fanned the inner flames.

His teeth closed over her earlobe, tugging gently, tenderly, until she murmured a low sound of pleasure. Releasing the flesh he'd held in erotic captivity, he said, "I think you know what I mean."

She knew she couldn't resist King any more than an avalanche, once under way, could halt its momentum. She'd tried. Truly she had. But being with King was like being swept along in a current so swift there was no hope of fighting its power. He overwhelmed her senses...and her good reason. She could only pray for the strength to hold back some small part of herself, to save a piece of her sanity that would allow her to go on without him as part of her life.

She angled her head to allow him easy access to the hypersensitive spot just below her ear. "You're very good at this," she said, her voice catching as his lips brushed against her flesh.

"At what?"

"Seduction."

"Where you're concerned, it's my favorite hobby," he replied, his tone a bantering smile. "Right after treasure hunting." He nuzzled the crook of her neck, nibbling lightly.

She shuddered and her breath came in a quick gasp.

A star appeared above the silhouetted mountains, the first star of the night, looking as though a bright spark from the fire had risen into the heavens. Margaret made her wish, that she could be first in King's life, but knew that dream wouldn't come true. She'd always play second fiddle to a new adventure, some irresistible quest that would draw him from her side. Just like her father. She fought off a desire to clench her teeth.

Tonight she'd feast on King. She'd devour each moment with him, each brush of his lips, the sweet flavor of his mouth and the salty taste of his skin. She'd store up memories. Like someone who feared a lifetime of deprivation, she'd indulge herself while she could. Tomorrow's chance might never come. She didn't dare risk what she already had.

Turning, she tangled her fingers in his hair and caught his mouth with hers. Heat. Scorching hot. Enough to burn the tactile memory into her soul. She vowed never to forget this feeling, never to regret this one moment in time.

She stroked her tongue along the moist, velvet seam of his lips, coaxing, rocking, until he became the aggressor, a low growl of need rumbling in his chest as he thrust against her intrusion. She gave way easily, realizing she'd gotten just what she'd wanted.

His deep probes sent sparks of fire darting all through her. Behind her closed eyelids a kaleidoscope of colors burst and twirled in a heated explosion of desire. These past few years her life had been only variations of gray. Now she detected myriad shades of light and dark, primary colors that took her breath away. And she wanted more. So much more.

"Oh, God, Maggie girl," he gasped, finally pulling away. "Do you know what you do to me?" The glow of the fire was a spark in the depths of his indigo eyes. The heat was within him, trying to get out, and she needed that fire to keep her warm against tomorrow.

"Show me, King," she ordered.

"Sweetheart." His raspy voice caught with emotion. "I'm no good for you."

"I know." The admission constricted her throat but she wasn't going to quit now. Her fingers went to the zipper of his jacket.

King had never known such madness. Or such gut-wrenching need. Was there any woman in the world more passionate than Maggie? He didn't think so.

He heard the nagging voice of his conscience telling him to leave her alone. But no warning in the world was strong enough to be heard over the desperate ache in his loins. Not when her delicate hands had already found their way under his long johns and were playing a seductive dance across his chest. Not when she sank her fingertips into his muscles and scored him softly with her nails. Not when her sweet taste was already on his tongue.

His deep-throated moan of pleasure was the sound of his conscience surrendering. His muscles clenched and corded beneath Maggie's exploring hands.

He captured the back of her head and pulled her down on top of him as he stretched them out on the sleeping bags. From her scalp to her hips he kneaded her body, molding her against him. He kissed her, a deep, seamless kiss that probed and tested, aroused and satisfied but did nothing to end the fiery ache that tortured him.

"Too many clothes," he murmured against her mouth.

"Making love in the summer—" she drew a shuddering breath when his palm finally found and cupped her breast "—is a lot less complicated."

"We'll find a way."

"I certainly hope so." An elemental need coursed through Margaret. As basic as the towering peaks that surrounded the valley, as natural as the need for survival in an unforgiving environment, the urge eroded what little of her good sense remained. Even the freezing mountain air as she stripped to bare flesh failed to dampen the burning flames that heated her from within.

She slid into the sleeping bag with King and he wrapped the softness around them, tugging her arced spine up hard against his chest. Bending her knees, she spooned herself along his length. As he nipped his teeth tenderly where her neck curved into her shoulder, one muscular arm underscored her breasts and his other hand delved through the curly thatch of blond hair that hid her womanhood, the source of a deep, throbbing sensation. She was distinctly aware of his hair-roughened thighs shifting against the smoothness of hers, her buttocks nestled at the lift of his hips, his long, tapered fingers caressing the excited nub between her thighs. Her breathing and heart rate accelerated beyond all control. In one shattering moment his arousal pressed against the nerve-rich area at the base of her spine.

A shock wave of desire exploded in her mind and body. The sensation rippled through her again and again as he rocked against her and his fingers circled her moist center.

Her breath lodged high in her throat, then escaped in a rush that became King's name on her lips.

"Easy, Maggie girl. Not too fast."

"It's not my fault. You're . . ." His fingers dipped into her and she no longer had a voice, or reason, to utter a complaint.

He locked his arm more tightly around her and made a sound that was thoroughly male. He was exquisitely masculine, every inch of him hard and demanding what she had to give. She wanted that, wanted to know he was climbing up the mountain with her and would teeter over the precipice with the same force that was driving her to the brink. She just wasn't sure how long she could wait.

King felt her tautness building. She was squirming against him, driving him crazy, just as her memory had left its mark on him all those years ago. It wasn't only that her inhibitions melted under his careful tutelage. More than that, she gave herself this willingly only to him. He sensed deep in his gut that no other man had ever aroused her quite so thoroughly—or received so much in return. The knowledge intoxicated him as if he were on a megadose of a performance-enhancing drug. He was high on Maggie. And painfully aware of how much he'd missed her...and would miss her again when all of this was over.

"King...I want to kiss you."

"My pleasure." He turned her in his arms, welcoming her lips as his hands explored the rest of her pliant body, her feminine curves and firm, sweet flesh.

Unable to resist the ultimate pleasure, he pressed himself into her, and the shock of heat splintered him, dragging a gasp from his lungs. "So good..."

"Yes..." she chanted. "Yes...yes..."

He drove harder, faster into her tightness. Blood thundered at his temple. His heart felt as though it might burst. He tried to wait, to hold on to the pleasure a moment longer, but then he felt her contract around him, squeezing him once, twice and again, her cries a sob in her throat, and he plummeted past the point of no return. The world tipped and spun out of kilter. He held on to Maggie, the only steady point in the reeling universe, and called out her name.

The stars spun for Margaret, too, a thousand pinpricks of light in a dark sky bursting with color. She accepted King's weight, gloried in it, and cherished the feel of their sweat-slicked bodies pressing together. She breathed in great gulps of cold air, as though she had raced up a mountain. The feeling was exhilarating, the need to force more air into her lungs a dizzying sensation.

When her heart slowed to a more rational beat and he pulled away from her, Margaret grieved the loss of his closeness. *Not yet,* she silently pleaded. She couldn't let him go so soon.

She snuggled next to him, draping one of her legs over his. His chest rose and fell rhythmically beneath her hand. Her fingers smoothed the crisp curls that roughened his flesh. With a sigh she caressed him with her lips and tasted his salt.

"Now will you let me sleep?" she asked, her arms and legs weighted with languor, her eyelids heavy.

"For about fifteen minutes. Then I'll have to check you again."

"King..." she complained. "Are you going to keep me awake all night?"

His hand cupped her shoulder, then slid down and around to caress the sensitive flesh of her inner arm. "It sounds like an excellent plan to me. If you'll cooperate."

She grinned. She'd nearly forgotten how insatiable he was. "Are you sure you're up to that?"

"I'll have to make the sacrifice," he teased. "In the interests of your good health, of course."

By dawn King had lost none of his enthusiasm for his task. Sometime during the night they'd moved the sleeping bags into the tent and zipped them together. The early-morning light gilded Maggie's body in an orange glow, like a golden treasure he could hold in his arms. Warm. Pliable. *His.*

He flicked his tongue across the flavorful indentation at the base of her throat.

"Hmm," she murmured, not fully awake.

"You taste good."

She shifted and stretched in the same sensuous way a purring cat greets the day. "I probably taste of you."

"Then it makes for a nice combination." He wove his fingers through her tangled hair, silver threads crowning her golden body.

Her eyes blinked open and she caught him smiling down at her with thoroughly masculine approval. "Don't you ever sleep?"

"Seems like a waste of time when there are more interesting things to do."

"Can't imagine what," she chided, her heart swelling with the joy of waking in King's arms. She was so filled with contentment her body hummed.

"If you don't know what I'm talking about, then maybe you're still suffering from that concussion."

"Perhaps you'd be willing to show me?"

"I'll certainly try."

And he did. Slowly, tenderly, until the sun was high in the sky and they were both sated.

SOME TIME LATER, Margaret came out of the tent to discover King already returning from his hunting expedition. The day was gloriously sunny with a temperature well above freezing. Only an occasional rumble in the distance suggested that the danger of avalanche had not yet passed.

"*Three* rabbits?" she questioned incredulously. He couldn't have been gone more than an hour. After he'd bungled putting up the tent the first time, she never would have guessed that he was such a skilled woodsman. "How did you trap them so fast?"

"I had some help," he admitted with a sheepish grin.

"Who? Where? Can they help us get back to civilization?"

He dropped the rabbits next to the cold fire. "I don't think so."

"Why on earth not?"

"He doesn't have that kind of power."

"He?" Margaret got a very discomforting sensation low in her belly.

"It's, ah, Whitecloud. He must have trapped them early this morning while we were, ah, busy...."

Slack jawed, she simply stared at King. He wasn't the kind of man who broke under pressure. At least, she didn't think so. "You want to run that by me one more time?"

"Well, see, it's a little hard to explain." He began the gruesome task of skinning the creatures he'd caught and Margaret had to look away.

"I'm listening."

"He seems to be haunting me."

"Oh, sure," Margaret groaned. What a crock!

She whirled back toward where King sat and glowered at him. "Tell me the truth, McDermott. You came across some skiers and paid them megabucks for those rabbits. You probably gave them unlimited credit on your gold card when you could have bought everything in their packs for a few dollars—like some yummy oatmeal, or even coffee—but you decided to impress me with your hunting skills."

"Hey, I don't understand what's happening, either. I walked out there—" he gestured over his shoulder ''—just like I did yesterday, and there they were. Rabbits. All nicely gutted and waiting. What was I supposed to do?''

Margaret sank to the ground. The poor man believed his own cockamamy story. ''We're going to be all right, King. I know we'll get out of this in one piece.''

''Sure. With Whitecloud's help.''

She rolled her eyes. Using her most patient voice, she said, ''Your friend Whitecloud is dead. You saw him shot. Remember?''

''I know that and I know none of this makes any sense. So maybe you can explain why a blizzard came up that was only five feet high, making the snow blow just enough to hide us when we should have been in Diane's... Tempest's... rifle sights.''

She shivered at the memory of how close they'd come to dying there on the mountainside. ''You think Whitecloud was responsible for saving us?''

''If it's not him, then my malaria has recurred and I'm hallucinating like I did in Peru. Except I don't have a fever this time. So I figure it's got to be Whitecloud.''

Worse and worse. ''He wasn't much help when we got creamed by the avalanche.''

''He says his Great Spirit powers are limited.''

Terrific! If she was going to have a ghost on her side, Margaret would have preferred an omnipotent one.

''I know it sounds crazy,'' King said, noting her dismay, ''but look at it this way. This was originally Indian country. The Indians were here centuries before white men showed up. Didn't these mountains have some religious meaning to the Miwoks? Supernatural stuff?''

"They were pretty primitive people in terms of their beliefs, at least from a modern point of view. Sort of a one-day-at-a-time philosophy. The Miwoks didn't have a creation story or even a major deity. But I suppose they must have held the mountains in some awe. Certainly they believed in a spirit world."

"So there you are." As though his conclusion should have been obvious to anyone with even an average IQ, King casually picked up a stick and spitted one of the rabbit carcasses. As hungry as she was, Margaret's stomach still threatened rebellion. Eating rabbit was one thing. Watching it skinned and skewered was quite something else. "Whitecloud has simply returned to the land of his ancestors," he continued, "and his spirit is helping us out. It's not that unusual. Those things happen in primitive cultures all over the world."

But not in Margaret's experience. Not ever. Perhaps she just hadn't traveled widely enough, she thought with a sigh that was half believing and half fearful King had slipped a cog.

"I'll find some more firewood," she announced, ignoring the catch in her voice.

"Great. And after we eat I'm going to make myself some snowshoes."

"So we can get back to Tuolumne?"

"Nope. I figure we can't be all that far from Whitecloud's cave. A day's hike at the most."

"You're not still determined to go after that damn treasure, are you?"

His lips tilted into a confident grin. "How can I miss with Whitecloud on my side?"

She sputtered and threw up her arms in defeat. The man was certifiable. For all of that, she couldn't change the fact that she loved him.

MARGARET EDGED THE KNIFE under the bark, trying for a narrow strip that could be used to lash the snow-shoe crosspieces together. Things weren't going well. Fortunately, all of her fingers were still intact, but she wasn't sure how long that would last, with the knife slipping more times than not.

She glanced across the fire to where King seemed to be having equal difficulty bending a slender pine branch into some semblance of a circle. He worked carefully, his hands moving with a casual but elegant grace. With an inward sigh she remembered how he had stroked and caressed her during the night. Even now, as his fingers worked so deftly, she could recall the fiery exploration of his hands on her flesh.

He might not be much at creating snowshoes out of raw material, but he was the most talented lover she could possibly imagine.

In fact, at this very moment she'd be happy to be back in his arms again.

Goodness, she mused, smiling to herself. She'd become as insatiable as King. Maybe this constant desire for lovemaking was contagious. She'd definitely caught King's spirit. Fortunately, he'd had enough foresight, as he had had in New Mexico, to come prepared with a large supply of condoms for such eventualities. Lord, she didn't even want to think about the possible consequences if King had been a less responsible man.

Studying King, she got a new flash of insight. The man was used to working alone. Except for Whitecloud, she'd never heard him mention any other friend or companion. Not even a woman, thank goodness. She wondered if that was by choice. Or had something about having a bodyguard in his childhood separated him from the chance to develop close personal relationships? An interesting possibility, she mused.

As she watched him at work, the branch snapped in his hands, in the same way the six previous tries had failed.

"It isn't working, King."

"We'll figure it out." He picked up another branch from those he'd gathered and began warming it over the fire in the hope of making it more pliable.

"I think we should be using willow, not pine." If and when she got back to the museum, she was going to have to pay more close attention to the exhibits.

"Probably, but it doesn't grow at this altitude."

He was quite an amazing man. Absolutely nothing seemed to faze him. Here they were in the middle of nowhere, at the mercy of the elements, their food provided by some Indian *spirit*, of all things. Their situation could go from bad to impossible at any moment, yet King sat there calmly trying to make snowshoes so he could continue his crazy treasure hunt. If Margaret hadn't known better, she would have thought King's life depended upon him finding those blasted gold coins. Yet he spent money as if it had no meaning at all.

"Why, King? Why is this treasure—any treasure, for that matter—so important to you?"

"It's not."

That didn't make any sense.

Having gained no insight at all into his motivations with that answer, she persisted. "Then why are we risking life and limb for some gold coins that may or may not exist?" The Indian museum was important to Margaret, but that couldn't be King's reason for continuing the hunt.

"Why not? As they say, it's a dirty job, but someone has to do it."

"That's what they say about cleaning out septic systems, not treasure hunting."

The newest dry branch broke in half and he tossed it casually aside, as though he hadn't a care in the world. "Ah, Maggie girl, as a kid I knew exactly what was going to happen every day. I was no better off than a prisoner with a life sentence. There was no challenge in that. No adventure. It's a pretty miserable way to live."

"Couldn't you have just taken up riding roller coasters if you were looking for fun? I mean, there are other exciting jobs a man can have besides chasing all over the world and getting shot at." Ordinary, *safe* occupations—like tightrope walking or flying experimental airplanes—where a man would have time for a wife and family.

"I don't need to work. Wouldn't know what to do with a job if I had one."

"Obviously you've lived a deprived life." She'd had her first job at age fifteen making take-out pizzas. Ever since, she'd hated the smell of tomato paste.

"Yeah. I suppose I have." He gave her an appraising look, one that did fluttery things to her midsection.

Crooking her a sexy grin, he stood and pulled Margaret to her feet. "Come on. I've got a better idea."

Why did she have the distinct impression King's ideas were carefully designed to get her in trouble?

Laughing, she ducked away from him. "Oh, no, you don't, McDermott. This time you're sticking to business. I don't plan to spend the rest of my life among the splendors of Yosemite. Let's go find some younger trees that are more pliable."

"You're a hard taskmaster, Maggie girl, when you know there are other occupations far more pleasurable for us to enjoy." Eyeing her with a mischievous twinkle, he took a couple of mock-threatening steps toward her.

In spite of his lighthearted teasing, Margaret retreated. In a way, his bantering personality was as much fun as actually making love. Well, maybe not quite *that* enjoyable, she admitted, aware of the pleasant tenderness between her thighs.

She headed off toward a nearby meadow in search of young trees and trying, for the moment, to keep out of King's reach. He laughed and joked, playing with her and knowing full well she'd give up the game soon enough.

High-altitude contrails streaked faint wisps of white across the cerulean sky. In the open areas the same sky blue color reflected back from the jumble of their footprints, almost as though they were running across an endless ocean. And the forest shone a deep, rich green, each pine needle sparkling in the sunlight as though washed by thoughtful winter storms.

Forgetting the playful chase, Margaret slowed and absorbed her surroundings with a sense of wonder.

"Oh, King, everything's so beautiful...." Or perhaps the world took on a special glow when she was with King.

She turned to smile up at him, only to discover he'd gone off on his own and was now digging in the snow.

"What are you doing?" she called to him.

"Making a snowman. Want to help?"

"Now?" She thought they were supposed to be making snowshoes. The man was certainly easily distracted. But then, with the trail blocked behind them by avalanches, an hour or a day's delay made little difference. She felt safe and strangely secure. There was no rational justification for that. Just that she was with King.

With a shrug she joined him. Within minutes the cold had penetrated her gloves, and a fair amount of icy snow had made its way past the collar of her jacket, helped along by a snowball or two that found their mark. King's warm laughter filled the silent forest and blanketed the meadow, then wrapped Margaret in a deep feeling of comfort she'd rarely experienced before.

King's concentration was not nearly so intent on making the snowman as Maggie might have suspected. Instead he was thinking about her.

Even knee-deep in snow she moved gracefully. She had the sexiest legs and the cutest little butt all tucked into those tight-fitting snow coveralls. He studied her slender figure, stunned by the rush of possessiveness that settled in his gut. She deserved a whole lot more than he could give her. Not just a casual fling every few years. Commitment. And all that it entailed. Something he didn't dare share with any woman.

Most of his life...with most of his relationships...he hadn't cared that there were only a few days, or nights, to worry about. He had a good reason to travel light, he told himself.

So why was Maggie different? And had been ever since Santa Fe? And why did the thought of walking away from her again hurt so damn much?

After they'd raised a life-size mound of snow, King said, "Now sit back, Maggie girl, and watch a master sculptor at work."

"I thought you were just supposed to put a couple of sticks in for arms and then a carrot nose."

"I never suspected you lacked creativity," he mocked. She sure as hell didn't in bed.

"One of my failings, I guess. Where I was raised in the San Joaquin Valley it usually rained sunshine most of the winter." She settled down in a sunny spot to watch him at work. He broke off a pine branch and used it much as an artist would, shaping the snow, smoothing and contouring the sculpture until she recognized—

"I hope that isn't a statue of me," she said with a giggle, jumping back to her feet. King's snowman was very definitely a snow woman with erotically formed breasts. "I'm not built that big!"

"Artistic license," he said, cupping his creations.

"You have a one-track mind." She laughed. Making love was definitely on her mind, too. King had a way of making her think about hot, sweaty bodies when she should be concentrating on getting safely back to civilization. "That's enough play time, King. We'll never get two pairs of snowshoes made if you can't keep your mind on business."

"Who says I'm making two pairs?"

"I do. You're not going to..." Her eyes widened in alarm. The man was going to do it again. "No, King, there's no way you're going to leave me behind."

"I can travel faster without you, sweetheart. I won't be gone long. That cave is probably just over the next hill, only a few miles from here."

"McDermott! I won't stand for—"

He stopped her complaint with a kiss, a deep, probing kiss that in moments had her gasping for air. He wouldn't really leave her, she thought dimly as she twined her fingers through the curls at the nape of his neck. She'd see to that....

Chapter Nine

Damn. Damn. Damn. In total frustration Margaret kicked at the cold remains of their fire.

King had made love to her all night long and then sneaked out of the tent before dawn while she still lay in exhausted sleep. Based on the oddly shaped footprints contouring the hillside, the snowshoes he'd finally jury-rigged from sapling pines were working just fine.

In contrast, the matching pair—*her* snowshoes that she'd insisted they make—had been ripped apart so she couldn't follow. At least, not easily. He'd made good on his promise that he'd go after the gold alone, finally claiming he didn't want to put her at risk again.

"Damn," she repeated under her breath. She'd never catch up with him now.

He'd left her and who knew when, or if, he'd ever come back.

She raised an angry fist at the threatening sky. When would she ever learn? Even now a light powdering of snow had begun to cover his footprints. The lunatic probably wouldn't be able to find his way back to her, assuming that was a part of his plan. As far as Margaret knew, King could have decided to keep the treasure for himself.

Sinking to her knees, she fought off the urge to weep. Of course he was coming back . . . this time.

No man could have made such exquisite love to a woman without caring about her. He wouldn't leave her stranded. Not in this godforsaken place without an airline ticket out. It simply wasn't King's style.

But leave her he would. That day would come. Sooner, rather than later, she imagined. God, it hurt. And there was nothing in the world she could do to change reality. No way would King allow himself to be trapped into an eight-to-five job, *trapped* into a marriage that meant putting down roots. He'd rather ride the crest of an avalanche than face a lifetime of mundane moments—like meat loaf every Monday night, like the soft gurgle of a baby, like a woman who was there waiting for him after a long day of work.

Her breath hitched.

Damn it all! That was what she wanted and that was what she'd have. With someone else, if that's what it took. She wasn't going to give her heart to King. Not all of it.

Just a big chunk, the insistent little voice in her head admitted.

She swiped the back of her hand against the press of tears. It would be nice if Whitecloud could conjure up a cup of hot coffee for her. She hated starting her day without a caffeine jolt.

Even the mountain silence grated on her nerves. How much better to have awakened in King's arms.

With a sigh she stirred the coals in the fire pit and tossed in a few twigs. Maybe later, after she fixed the snowshoes, she'd investigate the rest of the meadow. She'd seen a likely spot where she might find some edible bulbs hiding under the snow. Then she could roast them to provide variety for their diet, though she didn't expect them to be in the least tasty this time of year.

She was nibbling morosely on a bit of leftover rabbit meat when she heard the sound.

At first she thought it was another distant avalanche, but as the noise became louder and closer she looked up with considerable trepidation. It couldn't be King. He'd reported that their snowmobile was a total wreck. Besides, he'd headed off in the opposite direction.

Then again, the rugged mountains picked up sounds and bounced them back and forth, making it impossible to be sure of the source. The lowering clouds limited visibility.

Anxiety knotted her stomach. Diane's—or Tempest's—partner, if she had one, could be on their trail. On the other hand, it might be a search party trying to rescue them. Margaret's faithful museum volunteer could have become concerned....

Indecisive, Margaret stood and edged back under the sparse cover of the trees. The orange tent, however, was like a blazing candle. Anyone looking for them would be hard-pressed to miss it. If only it had snowed hard enough to camouflage the color, there might have been a chance to go unnoticed.

There seemed little point in running away. Her footprints would be obvious, and except for a small stand of trees there was nothing but open meadow. If she took off, they'd spot her in a minute. Racing through the snow did not appear to be a viable option for someone wearing an aquamarine snowsuit.

Darn King for leaving her all alone! He would have known what to do.

Swallowing hard, she looked around for a weapon. King had the hunting knife. The can opener, however ineffective, had been lost in the avalanche. All she could find was a heavy branch to use as a club.

The sound became more distinct—a rapid *thwack, thwack, thwack.* Her heart accelerated to the same rapid tempo. It didn't sound like any snowmobile she'd ever heard. Or anything natural. It had to be a...

Helicopter!

Looking like a giant red-and-white bird of prey, the helicopter skimmed along a hundred feet above the terrain. The roar was deafening. It banked slightly, the blades whirling, and headed right for the tent and the stand of trees where Margaret hid. For a crazy moment she thought King had arranged her transportation back home while he went on alone to his next adventure. Just like Santa Fe.

But that didn't make any sense.

The craft straightened and settled to the ground amid a self-made blizzard, the skids sinking silently into the cloud of snow the rotors had kicked up. The blades whipped slowly to a stop.

Margaret held her breath and her fingers tightened around her club. She prayed that real park rangers had somehow come to the rescue.

Cautiously someone opened the door. A figure appeared. Dressed in a flashy iridescent blue ski suit and matching cap, the man's slender physique was almost boyish. His gun wasn't.

"Oh, God," Margaret groaned. Smooth-Head Luke! How the devil had he found them here?

Struggling against a wave of panic, she looked around for somewhere to hide.

It was no good. The moment she budged he'd spot her. He was already scanning the area with his weapon at the ready, searching out every possible place to hide.

With little other choice, she decided to brazen her way through the difficult situation—*potentially fatal* situation, she mentally corrected, gritting her teeth.

The next time she saw King she'd have his head on a platter.

Stepping from behind the tree, she called, "Thank heavens you're here. I've been so frightened." Based on the way her heart was knocking against her ribs, she was indeed scared to death. And would probably stay that way until she got out of this mess.

At the sound of her voice, Smooth-Head whirled and the gun snapped toward her.

She let the club slip from her hand. It wouldn't do her an iota of good against his pistol. "I've been praying someone would—"

"Ms. Townsend?" he questioned.

"Yes, it's me, Mr. Luke." Knowing he was sensitive about his billiard-ball head, she wasn't about to get his dander up by using his nickname. "I'm so very grateful—"

"Where is he?"

"He?" she echoed, almost swallowing the word.

"Come now, Ms. Townsend, we have played hide-and-seek quite long enough." Smooth-Head came toward her, his strides amazingly unhindered by the deep snow. "You are far too intelligent to try to deceive me further."

For all of his short stature, Margaret realized he was a powerful man. And angry.

"You must mean King." She forced a weak smile. "He's not here."

"Then I trust you will inform me of his whereabouts. Immediately."

The fact that Little John had left the helicopter and was coming her way was a significant motivator. As if Smooth-Head's gun hadn't been persuasive enough.

Margaret's mouth went so dry her tongue felt like sandpaper. "He left."

"When?"

Casual conversation did not appear to be the man's long suit. *King really ought to cultivate a higher class of friends,* she thought, fighting off a bout of hysteria.

"He left yesterday," she bluffed. To her surprise her chin puckered and her lower lip quivered. Damn it all, she hadn't meant to cry. But she was so scared.... "He left me all alone. I'm not sure he's planning to come back." That wasn't entirely a lie. With King, a woman couldn't be sure.

"Oh, my dear...I had no idea you were suffering so." Luke's voice was filled with concern as he slid his gun back under his jacket. "McDermott is the most greedy of men but surely not even he would leave a beautiful woman stranded in such a desolate place."

Don't count on it. "We were attacked by a wolverine. I was afraid all night he might come back...." Stretching the truth came more easily than she had expected.

Luke placed a consoling arm around her shoulders. "We're here now, my dear. We shan't let anything hurt you. But you must tell us where King has gone."

"To look for the gold, I suppose."

"Yes. We know that. But where?"

She made a rather vague gesture toward the north, knowing that King had headed west. "He didn't let me get a good look at the map."

"My dear Ms. Townsend, you have obviously suffered at the hands of that scalawag but I must now pose a question which under other circumstances I would not consider asking. I want you to understand it is not like me to pry into another person's personal matters."

"Personal matters?" She didn't care for Smooth-Head's overly solicitous manner. It gave her a creepy feeling right down to the base of her spine.

"Quite so." He cleared his throat, his prominent Adam's apple shifting as he did. "Have you, my dear, been...shall we say...intimate with Kingsley McDermott?"

Heat raced up her neck. "Shall we say, it is none of your damn business?"

"A blush becomes you, Ms. Townsend, and also provides the answer I sought. You really must not lie to me, my dear. I do tend to become quite angry." His forehead wrinkled and his expression lost every bit of its earlier friendliness. He turned toward his companion. "Search the area, John. We'll make sure McDermott is not still lurking about. Then we will invite Ms. Townsend to accompany us on a short journey."

"I'm not going anywhere with you!" Among other things, this was the guy who had trashed her museum.

"Ah, but you are, my dear. And I have the utmost confidence your friend McDermott will attempt to rescue you."

"You're wrong, you know. King doesn't give a fig about me."

Luke's reed-thin lips quirked into an unpleasant smile. "We shall see."

A few minutes later Little John shoved Margaret into the back seat of the helicopter. She didn't go easily. Just before he slammed the door shut she cried, "King! Whitecloud! Do something!" At that moment Margaret would have been happy to conjure up every Indian spirit she could muster.

Before she could scream again Little John's big, meaty hand covered her mouth.

KING SLOUGHED THROUGH the snow. Things weren't going well. The jury-rigged snowshoes didn't work worth a darn. With his boots sinking into the snow at every step, it was like walking through six inches of molasses. Not his idea of fun.

Besides, if his calculations had been right, he should have found the turnoff to the Piute trail by now. Instead he seemed to have angled north, away from his destination. Of course, with the sky a gunmetal gray, it was hard to tell in which direction he was heading. His compass had been lost in the avalanche with much of the rest of the gear.

Just as well that he hadn't brought Maggie along. She wouldn't have been able to keep up. And stubborn woman that she was, she would have kept trying instead of giving up.

He smiled at the thought and felt his groin tighten. One hell of a lady, Maggie Townsend.

Wispy clouds dragged spindly tails along the tops of razor-sharp ridges, giving the mountains an ethereal quality and masking their shapes so King couldn't make out the landmarks. Not that he was lost, of course. But the map wasn't doing him much good.

He stopped to rest, only the sound of his labored breathing breaking the silence. The land was totally indifferent to his presence. Life was a fragile thing, the mountains seemed to say, and rarely endured for long.

The life of King's older brother had been briefer than most.

Richard Alexander McDermott III. Pride of the family. At the age of five Richie had lost his chance for a future. Then King had come along, a hasty replacement for the beloved older brother—albeit not nearly as intelligent nor quite so endearing as the first child, as King had been so often informed. His parents had thought to protect their younger child from the same kind of danger that had so cruelly snuffed out Richie's life. But in shielding King from every possible threat, they'd also strangled the opportunity for the challenge of each new day. Now, King made it a point to live hard enough and fast enough for both Mc-Dermott progeny. Not that he thought Richie would give a damn.

Drawing another deep breath that burned his lungs with the cold, King started forward again. One more treasure to find; one more challenge to conquer.

The tail of a cloud dipped into King's path, spinning in a threatening gray column of mist. King heard the distinctive rattle of Indian beads.

Mentally, he did a quick check of his health. No fever. No malaria. Just this strange recurring hallucination.

What the hell. He might as well go with the flow.

"Hey, Whitecloud. Is that you?" Maybe the guy had come to lead him to the cave. He supposed being haunted by the resident Indian had its advantages.

"You are a fool, my friend," came the harsh, disembodied voice from the cloud.

He shrugged. "Anybody can get lost. I figured you'd show up sooner or later." *Kind of like a desert mirage.*

"Getting lost is the least of your problems. Maggie is in trouble."

With a scowl King said, "She's all right. There's plenty of rabbit meat for her to eat, and she knows how to take care of herself."

"She is being kidnapped. Listen," the voice ordered.

King did. And heard the distant sputter of an engine trying repeatedly to catch in the thin mountain air. "Another snowmobile?"

"A helicopter."

Cursing, King whirled and started back the way he had come, running as fast as he could through the snow. He didn't need to ask who was piloting the whirlybird. Smooth-Head Luke had a hangar full of every imaginable kind of aircraft and knew how to fly them all. Little John was no doubt along for the ride to provide the muscle.

"You gotta stop 'em, Whitecloud!" King shouted over his shoulder. Mental aberrations ought to be good for something.

"I am doing the best I can." The cloud swirled up the trail ahead of King.

No way did King want Smooth-Head to take off with Maggie. There was something about the guy that really got to women. For a short little runt he could turn on the charm when he wanted to. Once King had asked a girl in Cancun about the strange attraction. She'd told him Smooth-Head brought out the mothering instincts in a woman.

Maggie, King suspected, had a lot of nurturing to give. And he'd be damned if he would let her share any of that with a bald-headed cretin who was trying to steal Whitecloud's treasure from him. And his girl.

He heard the engine backfire and then go silent. Maybe Whitecloud had stuffed a little snow into the intake manifold.

"Way to go, old friend," King said between gasping breaths.

Adrenaline pumped his legs harder, faster. He all but sprinted along the trail, at least as fast as the awkward snowshoes allowed. His lungs threatened to burst from exertion. Hearing the engine crank over again, King lengthened his stride. *Hang on, Maggie,* he mentally ordered. *I'm comin'.*

He crested a ridge and there was the helicopter right below him, the rotors spinning and stirring up a blizzard of loose snow. Through the side window he could make out Smooth-Head at the controls...and Maggie in the back seat. From the looks of things she was wrestling with Little John. For such a delicate woman she was one hell of a fighter.

The aircraft rocked and lifted a few feet off the ground. It hovered momentarily, as though the pilot was making sure the damn thing would stay in the air. A good idea, considering how difficult the engine had been to start.

Smooth-Head hadn't spotted King yet. The angle of his approach was too sharp to give good visibility. And Little John had his hands full with Maggie. He wasn't in a position to think about anything except the small fists that pummeled his shoulders.

King sensed as much as heard the angle of the rotors tilting and the acceleration of the motor.

Cursing aloud, he realized he was too far from the helicopter to stop them. He'd failed...and Smooth-Head and Little John had *his* Maggie in their clutches.

Slowly the helicopter rose another few feet, turned...and headed in King's direction.

There was only one thing left for King to do. He jumped as the helicopter passed over his head. With sheer determination he managed to hook an arm over a snow skid. He hung on, dangling beneath the helicopter as it gained altitude. The icy air bit into his cheeks and took his breath away. Frantically he tried to loop his other arm over the runner. The snowshoes acted like anchors dragging his feet back to earth.

Damn, he'd gotten himself into a real mess this time. He was a hundred feet above the ground and his right arm was being pulled out of its socket one painful ligament at a time.

Momentarily he thought about letting go, but quickly rejected the idea. He couldn't do that. Maggie needed him. With his quick temper, Smooth-Head was too damn unpredictable to chance leaving Maggie in his hands. Particularly if Maggie didn't give him what he wanted. And she wouldn't. King was sure of that. She was too stubborn for her own good. And, he suspected, more loyal to him than was healthy at this particular moment.

With a renewed surge of adrenaline he hauled himself up enough to grab the skid with his other arm. Then he just hung there like a kite tail beneath the helicopter, the wind battering him in the face as he tried to catch his breath.

This was going to be one hell of a ride.

The undulating terrain sped along beneath him. The cold wind brought tears to his eyes and King could only make out blurred images of steep canyon walls, ice-covered lakes and forested valleys. His arms lost all feeling. Blood coagulated in his feet like leaden boots. He ached and thought of Maggie and hung on. Time and direction became as ill defined as his vision. The roar of the motor assaulted his senses.

All he could do was vow that once on the ground again, he'd get Maggie to safety. He never should have involved her in the Yosemite caper.

Pine trees began to take on individual definition as the helicopter descended. In the distance King caught a glimpse of a small clearing and smoke drifting lazily up from a chimney. The pristine scene had to be someplace outside the park, but where?

Settling more rapidly, the copter skimmed the treetops so closely King drew his knees up as tight to his chest as he could manage. Crazy Luke! Didn't the man know it was dangerous to fly so low?

The aircraft banked to circle the cabin. King's eyes grew wide. The nut was going to fly right over a stand of the tallest trees around. . . .

King shouted a warning, but it was too late and probably went unheard.

The next thing he knew he was tumbling through the tops of a pine. Branches reached out to smash him in the face and on the shoulders; needles raked against him. He tumbled over and over. It was a hell of a long drop to the ground.

Chapter Ten

The rope cut painfully into Margaret's wrists where they were tied behind her back. The straight-backed chair was doing a number on her spine, too. And her stomach churned with fear for herself...and for King, who was God knew where in the mountains, not even aware she'd been kidnapped.

Not for a minute did she believe King would be able to rescue her from this predicament. Unless Whitecloud had an unlikely helicopter up his spirit sleeve. Which was a totally ridiculous notion. Her kidnappers had traveled too far, too fast for any man on snowshoes to keep up, even if he had known she needed help. This time she was on her own.

Smooth-Head Luke, in contrast, had a different idea. A tightly packed bundle of impatient energy, he was absolutely convinced King would show up at any moment and fall into his trap. He paced the one-room log cabin like a tiger in a cage. His agitation had escalated ever since they'd eaten a dismal meal of canned stew, and darkness had fallen.

Little John sat near the fireplace whittling a piece of wood. Margaret didn't like the way the big, bearded man eyed her from time to time, or just how skillfully he wielded his knife. *Deadly* was the word that came to mind.

Margaret swallowed uncomfortably.

"Tell me, Luke," she said, trying for a friendly, casual tone, as if she weren't terrified. "How did you know where to come looking for us?"

"It's very simple, my dear," Luke responded, at last stopping his restless movements around the room. "We heard a news report that two Yosemite rangers had been captured and bound up in a shed at Tuolumne Meadows. There'd been an impostor, we understood—"

"That wasn't King."

"Such a trick would not have been beneath McDermott, and as we were aware he was somewhere in the Sierras, we simply pursued the assumption that he would be at the source of any trouble within a three-hundred-mile radius."

"A reasonable assumption," she conceded with a wry smile. Obviously she had not been the only one to notice that King's middle name was Trouble.

"Indeed, the fact that the impostor was a woman was all the more reason to investigate the possibility of McDermott's involvement. Once we had determined you and he had been at the ranger outpost with a snowmobile, it was a simple process to search various quadrants of the wilderness area until we located your camp."

"All because a woman was involved?" Recalling how King had flirted with the mock ranger, and then how the woman had tumbled into the ravine, Margaret shivered. Not a pleasant memory, though she didn't feel a need to reveal the impostor's death to Luke. At least it confirmed that the real park rangers hadn't turned villains.

Shrugging his narrow shoulders, Luke held out his hands, palms up. His fingers were slender, his nails neatly manicured. "My dear, surely you do not believe you are the first woman whom he has despicably *used* in his nefarious schemes. Nor the first to succumb to his tales of adventure."

Probably not, she thought, hating the unbidden twist of jealousy she felt. But this was the last time—*positively the very last time*—she'd so much as go around the block with King. Assuming she got out of this mess alive.

"Would it mean anything to you if I said the woman who was masquerading as a ranger was named Tempest Storm?" she asked.

His eyes widened. Slowly he began to nod his head. "That explains a great deal, my dear."

"Then you knew her?"

"An employee. One who went missing shortly after Whitecloud let slip about the treasure."

Her jaw went slack with surprise. "You found out about the treasure from King's friend?"

"I fear Mr. Whitecloud didn't know he was being conned. It is an unfortunate weakness of his that I have often used to my advantage. Perhaps he also spoke out of turn in the presence of Ms. Storm."

"But that still doesn't explain... I don't even know how King knew where to find me." She shifted uncomfortably in the chair. "Or, for that matter, what brought you to my museum."

"That was the easiest deduction of all. When we heard of his friend's unfortunate death, we visited McDermott's home in Malibu."

"You weren't the ones who shot Whitecloud?"

Luke's gray eyes widened again, this time in shocked denial. "Certainly not, my dear. My code of ethics would not permit such rank amateur behavior." He made a series of *tsk*ing sounds. "Above all else, John and I are *professionals*. Although deaths may occur in this business, *murder* is simply not our style."

Then Diane—Tempest—had to be the guilty party, just as she and King had suspected. And Margaret would bet her last dollar that the growling German shepherd had belonged to the real rangers, not the impostor.

Margaret's gaze cut to Little John, and she wondered why she didn't feel a greater sense of relief that her two kidnappers didn't believe in murder. The big guy looked as if he'd be willing to spill a little blood at the least provocation. He'd already pricked her once with that big bowie knife and she didn't doubt he'd do it again, given the order. He'd yet to say word one. That gave her the willies as much as his knife. In any case, these two thugs had trashed her museum. She was still plenty mad about that.

"At McDermott's house," Luke continued, "we found several snapshots of you. Of course, they did not do you justice in my view."

Her gaze snapped back to Luke. "Pictures? Of me?" They had to be photos King had taken in New Mexico, but she'd never suspected he would have kept them all these years.

"Then there was a most interesting magazine, *The Curator's Quarterly,* I believe. A trade magazine, as you are no doubt aware. He'd obviously been a subscriber for some time, as though he had a particular interest in the business. Strange reading material for a man like McDermott, don't you agree?"

The curl of Luke's lips was a bit too knowing for Margaret's taste. Even so, she had to suppress a surge of pleasure. Could King possibly have been following her career? Maybe he *had* cared for her? It hardly seemed likely, and yet . . .

"McDermott had taken particular pains to circle an article describing the Sierra Indian Museum and its new young curator." He gave her a confident nod. "Since Whitecloud was an Indian and you the museum curator in question, we reached the obvious conclusion."

"I see." If King had been tracking her career, then that meant . . . But no, he could have called her anytime in the past five years and hadn't. He had known where to find her. Ergo . . .

She tucked the corner of her lower lip between her teeth. Luke was right. King had only wanted to *use* her expertise to find the gold coins. The fact that they had become lovers again meant nothing. Nothing at all. Except that she was a twice-foolish woman. Whatever she'd been feeling with King was no more than wishful thinking.

Double damn.

Luke resumed his pacing, glancing out the window into the darkness from time to time. John continued his relentless attack on a piece of pine. The shavings fell into the fire, caught and flared, then curled in on themselves. Margaret had the troubling feeling Little John would be just as happy peeling her skin off in exactly the same methodical way.

With renewed effort she tried to work her wrists free of their bindings.

"What sort of a trap have you set?" she asked, figuring if she managed to get out of the cabin she didn't want to get caught up in whatever they had in mind for King. Both Luke and Little John had spent several hours outside during the afternoon while she'd been inside trussed up like a Thanksgiving turkey.

"Oh, a little trick we learned in India," Luke replied. "No great harm will come to your friend, I assure you."

She raised a skeptical eyebrow.

"You've heard of tiger traps, of course."

The image of King falling into a deep hole filled with sharp wooden spikes leaped into Margaret's head and she drew a quick gasp. *Dear God, he'll be killed.* "I thought you said—"

"A large net, my dear," Luke interrupted with a faint smile, as though he'd read her mind. "If McDermott should try to enter the cabin, he will find himself swinging twenty feet off the ground. He'll be quite safe, of course, but helpless. I should think under the circumstances he would be willing to share the map with us, or the coins, if he has discovered them."

"I'm sure he'll be delighted," she said under her breath. "Exactly where are these nets you mentioned located?" she added aloud.

He *tsk*ed at her again. "Now that would be giving the game away, wouldn't it?"

Treasure hunting was definitely not Margaret's kind of game. A few rounds of cribbage in front of a cozy fire was far more her style. Evidently King, Luke and John all shared a lack of interest in such a safe sort of challenge.

THE SCENT OF WOOD SMOKE drifted through the pine forest. King avoided the square of yellow light that spilled out of the cabin onto the snow. Moving at all wasn't easy, much less with enough caution so Smooth-Head and Little John wouldn't catch sight of him. Or hear him.

King's ankle hurt like the very devil, and every time he drew a breath his ribs complained. None of that mattered. It was the way a heavy load of guilt rested on his shoulders that really bothered King.

He never should have involved Maggie in this dangerous business of treasure hunting. Her sweet, soft little body was too precious to take these kinds of risks.

That he had broken his vow of never seeing her again suggested old age was creeping up on him. From now on he'd definitely have to watch his step.

King hunkered down behind a tree to catch his breath. He didn't dare think too hard about the woman tied up in the cabin. Or how much he'd miss her once he'd gotten her out of this mess. Those kinds of thoughts would only distract him from what he had to do.

BLOWING OUT A LONG SIGH, Margaret twisted in her chair and wondered if Luke would ever let down his guard. She'd likely get only one chance to escape. When she did, she'd better make it good.

She was just contemplating making a request to visit the outdoor facilities, and then making a break for it, when she heard the first shout.

"Damn it, Smooth-Head!" King's voice thundered. "Let me outta here!"

"Oh, no," Margaret groaned. Somehow King had managed to track her down and then he'd gotten himself caught. Her throat constricted.

"At last our reluctant hero arrives!" Luke announced, sounding like a smug bantam rooster. Both he and Little John raced for the door.

A blast of cold air flooded the room as the two kidnappers ran outside.

"Fool! Fool!" she whispered, her witless heart swelling with the love she couldn't repress and her eyes pooling with tears. She would have managed on her own. King didn't have to risk his stupid neck just to rescue her.

"Boss! Boss!" came a high-pitched, feminine-sounding scream. "He's got me!"

With a clench of her teeth and a suspicious frown, Margaret wondered what on earth King was doing with a woman.

"King! You're not playing fair," Luke bellowed.

Tell me about it, Margaret mentally agreed. Women flocked to the man the same way danger did.

There was so much shouting and swearing going on, a fair share of it in that strange, squeaky woman's voice, Margaret couldn't figure out what was happening. She squirmed and struggled against her bindings. The rope only chafed her wrists more deeply. And the thought that the woman King had brought along was an "intimate" friend rubbed even more deeply into her wounded pride.

In her struggle she managed to tip over her chair, and she landed hard on her shoulder. Pain arrowed down her arm. "Darn it all!" she cried, choking back a sob as she tried to kick free of the chair. "Somebody tell me what's going on."

She rolled around on the splintery floor and then came nose to toe with a large black boot. Slowly, her heart in her throat, she raised her gaze. Amused silver-blue eyes looked down at her.

"King . . ." His name escaped her lips in a relieved sigh. Realizing she shouldn't be all that glad to see him, Margaret tensed. "How did you get here?"

"It's a long story, Maggie girl." He rubbed his palm along his jaw, wincing as he did. "I'll tell you about it later. Now I think I'd better get those ropes off you. I'm not sure how long Smooth-Head will be tied up."

"They had a trap set for you."

Kneeling, King turned her so he could work at the knotted rope that bound her wrists. "I know. That's what took me so long. I had to rearrange the little surprise they'd planned for me."

"You mean they were caught in their own—"

"From the sound of it, they're not too pleased about being snared." A smug grin curled his lips. "Smooth-Head should have come up with somethin' new instead of trying to nail me with that old stunt I used on him in India."

Shaking her head, Margaret rubbed her chafed wrists. The man was incorrigible. "So what about your new girlfriend? Is she going to get us out of this place?"

He gave her a puzzled look. "What girlfriend?"

As King helped Margaret to her feet, she said, "King, that mezzo-soprano is hardly a well-kept secret. She's screaming her head off. I've never heard such a screeching voice. It's like fingernails scraping on the blackboard." Though come to think of it, if the woman and King were together, why was she yelling so loudly?

King's roar of laughter caught her off guard. "Sweetheart, that's not a woman. That's Little John."

She did a mental double take. "You're kidding. That huge hairy bear of a man—"

"That's why he doesn't talk much. Kinda sensitive on the subject, I imagine." He took her elbow. "Let's get outta here before those two guys figure how to get out of the cargo net they're strung up in."

Margaret felt a definite sense of déjà vu. King was always on the run from someone. Lately, so was she.

They stepped outside to an ominous silence. The cargo net hung empty.

"Son of a gun!" King grabbed her hand and they ran toward the clearing where the helicopter was parked. He limped with every step, his breath hissing through his teeth as though he was in considerable pain.

For the moment Margaret had her own problems making her legs respond to her commands. But she didn't like the way King was struggling with every step.

When they reached the helicopter he yanked open the door and shoved her inside, following right behind her. Breathing hard, he collapsed into the pilot's seat. In the dim light Margaret could see sweat beading his forehead. A long red scratch creased his cheek.

"What's wrong, King? You're hurt."

"Had a little trouble with my landing."

"What does that mean?"

"It means Smooth-Head is a lousy pilot and he almost got me killed when he flew too close to the treetops." King fiddled with the controls. "I fell off the damn skids and a tree kinda got in my way on the way down. I'll be okay."

She looked at him incredulously. "You were hanging on beneath the helicopter all that time?"

"How else was I supposed to rescue you?"

Suspicions confirmed—the man was crazy. She felt a tightness in her chest. He could have died doing a stunt like that.

"I suppose you're planning to set the bones yourself?" she asked in exasperation, both at King and the sudden weepy feeling that threatened to overtake her.

"I don't think anything's broken." He leaned forward to switch on the ignition and winced. The rotors slowly began to turn. "Maybe a bruised rib or two."

"King, let's call this whole thing off. Just this once let Luke win the game...that's what you lunatics think this is all about. A game. You need to see a doctor and have X rays taken.'' No museum in the world was worth King's life.

As usual he ignored her plea. Instead he wobbled the controls back and forth. From Margaret's point of view he looked a bit unsure of himself. That gave her a familiar queasy feeling in the pit of her stomach.

''You do know how to fly this thing, don't you?''

''Sure. No problem.''

She'd thought as much. ''That's it, King. I'm gone. No way am I going to fly in a helicopter with an unlicensed pilot. I'll take my chances with—''

A bullet exploded through the cockpit, shattering the plastic canopy.

Margaret screamed and covered her ears. ''Luke claimed he never killed anyone!''

''Here we go,'' King calmly announced as he did whatever it was that made helicopters go up.

By the time they rose above the treetops, the thudding sound of bullets penetrating the fuselage had stopped. Margaret found she was trembling. Maybe it was just the erratic motion of the helicopter, she told herself. The wild rides at Disneyland weren't her cup of tea, either. She held on to the edge of her seat. Her stomach did little flip-flops with each bouncing movement. It was almost too much for her to handle.

''Do you have any idea what misery you've put me through the last few days?'' she complained.

''It gets better and better, doesn't it?'' He gave her a weak imitation of his cocky grin and she realized he was in serious pain. The man had gone to who-knew-what lengths to save her, risking his own neck in the

process. She supposed she ought to be grateful for
that.

Margaret glanced out of the cockpit to see scattered snowflakes sliding by the window in the reflected light of the control panel. The night was really
dark. Not a single star shone in the sky. And no lights
were visible on the ground.

"King, do you have any idea where we're going?"

"Not exactly."

The few gauges on the control panel weren't very
revealing, particularly those covered with stickers
reading In-Op. Luke had evidently let the mainte-
nance of the helicopter slip rather badly.

"I know there aren't any cabins within the bound-
aries of the park," Margaret said. "That means we
have to be east of Yosemite, which should put us pretty
close to Nevada." And something resembling civilization. "If we just keep going east until we get out of
the mountains, I'm sure we'll see the highway."

"Sounds reasonable to me," King agreed. He
tapped the compass with his knuckle. "Problem is,
this damn thing seems to be frozen."

"So we could be going any direction?"

The grim set of his lips was all the answer she
needed.

Hysteria threatened. "King, let's land this thing. We
can call for help on the radio. Surely someone will
come to our rescue." She lifted the microphone and
fiddled with the dial.

"If you're going to send a Mayday, you'd better
hurry. We're going to be landing much sooner than I
had expected."

"What are you talking about?"

He pointed at the gas gauge, which registered nearly empty.

"Oh, my God," she groaned.

"I think one of Smooth-Head's shots caught the gas tank. That dial's been falling pretty fast ever since we took off."

Now that he'd mentioned it, Margaret could smell gasoline. The fumes suddenly made her sick to her stomach. The thought of the helicopter going up in a burst of flames added to her nausea.

She keyed the microphone. "Help. Please... Is anyone listening? We're going to crash." Each plea scraped painfully up her throat.

The engine sputtered. Like an express elevator going down, the helicopter gave up a hundred feet of altitude before King's wobbling of the controls had any effect.

Margaret stifled a scream.

Below them was nothing but inky blackness. Snowflakes accelerated their flight past the cockpit window. Wind buffeted the helicopter.

"Please," she cried into the mike. "We're out of gas. I don't know where we are." *Or if we'll both be killed in the next two minutes.* "Mayday. Mayday."

The engine cut out again. The rotors freewheeled.

"We're going in, sweetheart. Lean over, put your head down between your legs and hold on tight."

In an instinctive gesture she reached for King's hand. She felt him squeeze her fingers just before the impact jarred her senseless.

Chapter Eleven

Like icy fingers a cold wind slid through the broken fuselage. The crash had ripped the tail section from the helicopter; a tree branch had speared the windshield, missing Margaret by inches. The radio dangled from a single wire, its innards shattered.

She shrugged off a sheet of Plexiglas that had fallen into her lap. "Now I suppose you're going to tell me we're really having fun."

"Maybe *fun* is a poor choice of words," King conceded, lifting her hand and placing a soft, warm kiss on her palm. "You okay?"

"All in one piece," she said on a sigh.

Leaning her head back against the seat, she wondered how they had both survived the crash. The helicopter had turned into a twisted metal puzzle that was hardly recognizable as a flying machine. She'd never been so scared in her life. Her heart was still doing a good imitation of a sprinter's beat in her chest.

Yet never had she ever felt quite so alive as she did at that moment.

The wind through the trees seemed particularly eerie, as though she could distinguish the movement of each pine needle as it shifted on the branch. She could feel individual snowflakes land on her face, slowly warm and melt, dampening her cheeks like miniature tears. The seat molded to the shape of her body as though specially designed for her. She was aware of her breathing, the rapid rise and fall of her chest, the cold air that dragged through her lungs.

But most of all she was acutely conscious of King— the way he still held her hand, the rough whiskers on his face, his musky, masculine scent that not even the icy wind could disguise. His easy confidence.

Miracle upon miracles, they were both alive.

She wanted nothing more than to validate that truth by being in King's arms.

So much for her vaunted resolution to strangle him at her very next opportunity.

The fact that her feelings toward King vacillated so wildly frightened Margaret. Normally she was a pretty steady person. She liked to analyze and plan ahead, have her days carefully cataloged. She preferred order in her life, not the chaos that King managed to engender, creating a tug-of-war between her head and her heart.

Why was it that no other man had kept her so off balance? She'd dreamed of settling down with the equivalent of a nice, stodgy bookkeeper. Instead, she was drawn to a lunatic who could have made a fortune bottling and selling the extra adrenaline his antics kept pumping through her veins. Life simply wasn't fair.

King held himself very still. He'd sworn not to lay another hand on Maggie. He'd done enough damage already. He'd practically gotten them both killed.

In the face of that, she looked downright calm. One sassy little remark, then she'd settled into a sexy pose with her head tilted back, her lips relaxed and slightly parted, and he was going crazy wanting to kiss her.

He was really scared now. Scared for her that he'd do something foolish. Again.

The snow was beginning to form a pile on the cockpit floor beneath the shattered windshield. Even knowing the helicopter no longer offered adequate shelter from the increasing storm, it took all of King's willpower to release Maggie's hand and get them moving.

"We've got to find someplace to hide out from the storm," he said. "I noticed Smooth-Head had a couple of packs in the back. There ought to be a tent and some emergency supplies."

"Shouldn't we stay close to the wreckage in case someone heard our radio message?"

"We will." Though King didn't think there was much point. Their altitude had been well below the surrounding mountain peaks when she'd sent the radio signal. It seemed unlikely anyone had heard their Mayday. After the storm passed they'd have to find a way out of the mountains on their own.

He shoved open the cockpit door and stepped out into the wind. His sprained ankle zinged him a good one the first time he put any weight on it.

"You'd better let me get the packs," Maggie insisted as she joined him beside the helicopter. "You're in no condition to walk, much less carry any extra load."

"I'm okay." He limped toward the broken tail section.

"Don't be so macho. It'd be better if you could find someplace where we could get in out of this wind. I think the temperature is falling, too. Looks like we're in for a full-fledged blizzard."

Damn. As much as King hated to admit it, Maggie was right. The weather was closing in fast.

The snow whipped around his face, limiting visibility. During the quick glimpse of the terrain he'd gotten before the crash, he'd spotted the rugged outline of a hillside off to the left. Then they'd landed in the trees that marked the base of the outcropping of rock. They'd either have to set up camp among the trees, using them as a windbreak, or find some kind of shelter in the rocks. In either case, they'd likely spend a damn cold night.

But to his surprise, luck was finally with them.

Right at the base of the boulders King found the entrance to a cave half-hidden by a fallen tree. Dragging a pack behind him, he crawled inside. His bruised ribs were giving him fits and the cold seemed to be settling into his ankle, making it painfully stiff. With shaking hands he managed to strike a match.

"I'll be darned," he said as the flame burned down to his fingertips. The cave was big enough to stand in and went back farther into the rock than the light of a single match could reach. "Come on, Maggie girl," he shouted. "I've found us a nice, cozy spot."

Margaret propped the two pairs of cross-country skis she'd found in the helicopter next to the cave entrance and then dropped to all fours. The pack on her back weighed a ton. She hoped King was right about cozy. Warm would be nice, too. Currently unoccupied by any wild creatures would be a plus.

She wormed her way inside and was greeted by the welcoming glow of a small fire made of twigs and leaves.

King grinned at her. "How's this for going first-class?"

The Palm Springs Hilton would have been an improvement but she supposed this was better than she could have expected, given the circumstances. She knelt beside the fire and held out her hands to warm them. The whistling of the wind outside had dropped to a low, keening sound.

"Heaven," she said, smiling back at King.

She held his gaze and felt a quick surge of adrenaline kick in at the same time she was suffused with a feeling of crazy, illogical love. Lord help her, she didn't seem able to fight the feeling.

King swallowed, caught by the tempting warmth in her eyes, and for just a moment it lured him. He forgot how he'd thoughtlessly exposed Maggie to unnecessary risks. More times than once, he admitted. He forgot his past, too, the danger that being tied to him would represent to any woman... and the children a woman like Maggie would naturally want. He let slip from his mind the prison his childhood had been and thought only of the pleasure of waking up each morning with Maggie in his arms.

But memories, reality, had a way of sneaking back where they belong, he reminded himself firmly.

With a mental curse he broke eye contact. Keeping the fire going with the twigs and sticks some animal had used to make a nest became a high priority.

Margaret experienced a painful and unexpected sense of loss when King turned away. She'd seen something in his eyes she hadn't noticed before. There'd been no bright, bantering light reflecting back at her. None of the spark she'd grown to love. There'd been only crushing hurt and a deep-seated loneliness. But how was that possible?

"King, what's wrong?"

The fire flared as he dropped some dry leaves into the center of the stone circle. "We'll be okay. The storm won't last long and we've got plenty of supplies. I'll get you out of here safe and sound."

"But what if I don't want to go?" she asked, frowning at his strange behavior and cocking her head.

"Trust me, sweetheart. You want to get as far away from me as possible, just as fast as you can."

Her throat clogged with denial. "Why?"

"Because I'm no good for you. That ought to be pretty obvious by now."

"I think I'm capable of deciding what's good for me," she insisted, angry that her voice had developed a catch. "Besides, why the sudden change of heart? You've spent the last several days trying to seduce me. Quite successfully, I might add. Now you're all set to haul me back to the safety of civilization. Why, King? What's changed?"

"Reality intrudes," he grumbled.

"I'm not going to accept that as an answer. For the second time I've fallen head over—" She didn't dare admit the full range of her emotions to King. He looked far too vulnerable, as though he was quite ready to flee rather than fight. "Tea kettle and you're talking about reality? Surely I deserve a better explanation than that."

He stirred at the fire with a long stick, his expression pensive. "I suppose you're right."

She angled her legs into a more comfortable sitting position. The glow of the fire warmed her face and the storm outside seemed as though it were badgering another world. "I'm ready to listen."

Dropping his stirring stick into the fire, he glanced up at her. Instead of silver-blue, his eyes were dark, their color flat and unreadable. "Did you ever hear about the McDermott kidnapping? More than thirty-five years ago?"

She searched her memory. "Maybe. I think there was a TV movie. Something about a newspaper publisher?"

"You got it. That was my dad."

"Your father publishes the—"

"He died. My name's on the masthead now. The title brings with it a lot of notoriety, not that I've actually been around the office in the last fifteen years or so."

"But I thought... Didn't the kidnapped child die?"

"My older brother, Richard Alexander McDermott III. He was five at the time. They had me about a year later as sort of a consolation prize." His words were sharp edged with pain that he'd carried a long time.

"You can't mean—"

"All I know is that my folks turned the house into a mausoleum dedicated to Richie's memory—the perfect son who had died too young. They made me tiptoe around the place like I was carrying some kind of virus."

"Their grief must have been unbearable."

"Hey, I understand what they went through." He scooped up some more twigs for the fire. "They certainly explained it often enough. And they did everything they could to prevent the same kind of thing happening to me."

A lot of the puzzle pieces that made up Kingsley McDermott were beginning to come together for Margaret. "Were there threats on your life?"

"Sure. With a family as prominent as ours, there are a lot of copycats out there who would love to cop a few headlines. Real creeps."

"Psychotics."

"Probably. And entirely capable of following through with their threats."

"That must have been terrible for you, growing up knowing someone wanted to kill you."

"I still get threats, Maggie. You have to understand that. They come to the newspaper, and sometimes to the family estate on Lake Michigan. One or two a month. All asking a million dollars or so. Most of them are from crazies but you can't entirely ignore them."

Margaret stared into the fire feeling sick to her stomach. How could anyone live a normal existence with that kind of sword of Damocles hanging over their head?

"They've even threatened my wife and my kids."

Her head snapped up.

"I've never been married, Maggie. And I don't intend to. I wouldn't put any woman through that. The constant threats all but killed my mother. As it was, she was a mental basket case. It was a blessing when she finally gave up and simply died."

Never marry? Was this the *trap* he had talked about? Not for him but for a woman? "But what if you found a stronger woman? Someone who could handle—"

"No one can withstand that kind of pressure and survive. Think about it, Maggie." He arrowed her an intense look that penetrated past any bravado she might offer. "How would you cope if your children were always under the threat of some nut who wanted to kidnap them?"

The whole concept was nearly beyond her comprehension. The original kidnapping had taken place more than thirty years ago. Yet King was still a victim...a victim of the maniac who had killed his brother and a victim of his parents' fear and grief. Little wonder he was a rolling stone.

"I don't know how I'd act," she admitted, her voice hoarse with emotion. All she knew was that she wanted to take King in her arms, hold him, convince him that tomorrow would be all right, even when she suspected that was far too simplistic a response.

He finger-combed his hair in a rough and careless way. "Let's get some sleep." He reached for the pack he'd dragged into the cave and unlashed the sleeping bag that had been strapped to the top. He spread it next to the fire. "I'll try to keep the fire going during the night. You'll be warm enough in your bag."

Margaret had every intention of staying warm, but not alone. She took her bag from the second pack and spread it out next to the first. With a few deft movements she had the two bags zipped together.

"What are you doing?" King asked.

"Looks downright comfy, doesn't it?" She stood back to appraise her handiwork. "Nice of Luke to arrange five-star accommodations for us."

"What you have in mind is not a good plan."

"Twenty-four hours ago you certainly thought it was." She gave him a smug grin as she shrugged off her jacket and then tugged her wool sweater up over her head.

King swallowed hard. How was a guy supposed to keep his new hands-off resolution when she was doing a seductive striptease right in front of his face? He watched as she tossed her boots aside. Her pants went next, sliding slowly down her thighs as she did some kind of a sexy twist of her hips.

"Maggie..." he warned hoarsely. The lump in his throat had grown to about baseball size. He also had a painful complaint about a different, lower part of his anatomy.

"Because of you I've spent the last few days getting battered and bruised. You're not going to add insult to injury by letting me freeze my buns off all alone, are you?''

No, he wouldn't want any part of her silken body to freeze on his account. "But my ribs," he protested, still trying to make the ultimate sacrifice of self-denial. "I'm not sure I can—"

"Are they broken?"

"I don't think so, but—"

"Good." Her predatory grin gave him a start. "Then I'll be on top and you'll be just fine. I'll be gentle," she promised in a low, husky voice.

King failed to stifle a groan. Those hazel eyes of hers were looking at him with golden sparks of devilment that were damned hard for a guy to resist. As she sauntered toward him, hips swaying, long blond hair brushing her shoulders, he forgot how to breathe. Internal fires began to build somewhere deep in his gut. Martyrdom didn't suit him, he decided.

His arm snaked out, coiled around her slender waist and dragged her hard against his chest. "You're asking for trouble, Maggie girl."

She gasped and shivered a little. "I know," she whispered. For a moment the stubborn bravado left her eyes and King saw the depths of her vulnerability. But it was too late for him to stop.

He brought his lips down hard and hungry on her mouth.

At the first contact of his hot, moist lips, Margaret went on the attack. She would have this man. Now. For these few minutes or hours, huddled together within a smoky cave, she would love Kingsley McDermott. Damn the raging storm outside and all the tomorrows she'd have to face alone. For now she'd tame the tumult within her.

She plunged her tongue between his lips, tasting and demanding, caught up in the sensations that rippled wildly through her entire body and those that were echoed in the shudder of King's shoulders. She clutched at him, drove her fingers through the waves of his hair and heard a low, throaty groan that could have been his or hers.

But he was no passive lover. King crushed Maggie to him, his hands splaying along the curve of her back, searching for the elastic at her waist, then ripping her long johns down around the curve of her hips and tearing the undergarment from her legs. In almost the same motion he dropped his pants to his knees then dragged her back to him. Standing with legs spread wide apart for balance, he cupped her buttocks until he could lift her off her feet. Automatically her legs locked around his waist.

"Oh..." she cried.

"There's trouble for you, Maggie girl."

"Yes... Oh, yes." He pressed her hard up against the cave wall and she clung to him, making sobbing, hungry sounds as he rotated his hips and thrust into her. Her silken legs were like a powerful vise pulling him deeper inside. She took every inch of him and seemed to be asking for more.

He'd never known such mindless heat. Such unbearable pleasure.

The coals in the fire pit cast flickering shadows across the cave wall and gilded Maggie's face in a passionate glow. He stroked her supple body, inside and out.

Margaret felt the tension building within her, rising beyond the point of control, a conflagration of heat and passion that knew no bounds—a violent storm raging toward the brink of self-destruction. She didn't want the feeling to stop, yet the ache was so intense she knew she would go mad if it went on much longer.

Even so, the explosive relief caught her off guard. She threw back her head, arching her back, crying King's name on a broken sob. Her scream echoed through the empty cave, crying out again and again as her body spasmed in rapid, repeated contractions.

He pulled her head down to rest on his shoulder again. Her moment of quiet had a dreamy quality, her breath a soft, raspy breeze, no longer so stormy. He carried her the few short steps to their sleeping bags, still within her, lowering her with him until she lay across him as though they could never be separated again.

On a sigh, she softly placed little kisses on the side of his neck, tasting his salty flavor, cherishing his musky scent. Impossibly, inside her she felt him grow. With a hungry groan she kissed the scratch on his face while she tenderly caressed his bruised ribs. The heated pressure grew within her.

"My turn, sweetheart," he said, his hands lifting her head so he could look into her eyes.

"My pleasure." The way he filled her, giving her a total sense of completeness, Margaret was sure the second time around would be even more wildly satisfying than the first.

She braced herself on his shoulders while his hands slipped to her waist. She rode him, matching him thrust for thrust, matching his rhythm, surrounding him with searing, gripping heat.

"Maggie, Maggie," he cried, dragging her back down into his arms. His body pulsated; his shoulders shook.

In an incredible moment she joined him in a flight over a precipice so high, so exquisitely fragile that she was vividly aware of time and space, scents and sounds, the brilliant colors of a rainbow and emotions that might well never be held in check again.

Chapter Twelve

In the morning the storm was still whipping snow across the landscape.

From the warmth of her sleeping bag Margaret gazed up at the rocky ceiling of the cave. In the dim light she could see the sooty evidence of a good many fires the previous occupants had built. Over how many generations had people taken shelter from storms in this very spot? she wondered. The thought that a few might have made love with the same wild abandon that she and King had all during the night brought a satisfied smile to her lips.

Now that she thought about it, she had spread out their sleeping bags in an area beside the fire that had been cleared of rocks and smoothed by prior use. The firewood they'd used was so handy it was as though someone had expected to return to his favorite camping place soon.

A frown tightened her forehead.

Moving carefully so she wouldn't awaken King, she slipped out of the sleeping bag. Goose bumps rose on her bare flesh and she hurried to pull on the clothes she'd scattered haphazardly around the cave last night. She smiled again at the memory of her wild, reckless behavior and King's enthusiastic response.

They'd always been good together.

Stirring the banked coals in the fire pit, she got the fire going again and made a crude torch from a bunch of sapling branches and leaves.

Curiosity and a second sense guided her toward the back of the cave. The way narrowed and she was forced to duck her head. The sight of another sooty streak on the rocks brought a flutter of excitement to Margaret's stomach. It might have been left there by some cross-country skier only a week ago... or by a traveler from another century.

Indians? That was a possibility.

Indians with a million dollars in gold coins? The odds weren't exactly good. Still...

The air smelled musty this far back in the cave and her light flickered, casting odd shadows along the rugged walls in a way that gave her an eerie feeling, as though the place had once been inhabited by spirits from another world. The dirt beneath her boots was a fine, powdery dust, rising in a silent puff each time she took a step.

Her foot slipped on a rock she hadn't noticed and she reached out her hand to balance herself against the side of the cave.

Then she saw it.

Her breath caught. *Oh, my God....*

Kneeling, she adjusted her torch to get a better look.

On the back wall of the cave a smooth slab of granite bore unmistakable markings, ancient graffiti depicting an antlered deer leaping over the head of a long-eared rabbit. Her fingers trembled as she reached out to touch the primitive drawing . . . thinking of the Indian brave who had no doubt tried his artistic skills here . . . then she quickly withdrew her hand when she realized her body oils would damage the petroglyphs.

What a find! she thought in wonder. Far more exciting in her view than any stash of nineteenth-century gold coins. The discovery would put the Sierra Indian Museum on the map, assuming she could afford an outside expert to authenticate the drawing and find a way to keep the organization from bankruptcy after repairing the damage that Luke had done to the displays. If she could pull it off, there'd be journal articles to write and a thorough archaeological investigation to supervise, all of which would require new funding sources. She'd probably be asked to speak at the next curators' conference.

If Margaret had thought she'd been overworked before, without enough hours in the day to get everything accomplished, now she knew she would be swamped.

A hysterical chuckle chortled up from her throat. "Like everything else that happens with you, Kingsley McDermott, this is definitely a mixed blessing."

"Hey, what's going on back there?" King called from the main part of the cave.

"I've discovered something interesting."

"Like what?" he questioned.

"Come see for yourself, and bring another torch. This one has just about burned out." Margaret would be the one burned out by the end of the year. Or unemployed.

King heard the excitement in her voice and wondered what was going on. He found a flashlight in Smooth-Head's pack and used it to guide him toward Maggie's voice. As the cave narrowed he thought he heard the distinctive rattle of Indian beads.

He halted abruptly. There was no sign of Whitecloud, but his old buddy had to be there . . . or, rather, his spirit. The hairs on the back of King's neck always reacted with that same creepy feeling when the Indian showed up.

This whole business with Whitecloud was spooky. King wondered how to go about getting himself unhaunted. Or maybe, just maybe, Whitecloud was sending another message, one that was tough to read.

Ducking under a low outcropping of rock, King reached the end of the cave and Maggie. "What's up?"

"Shine your flashlight over here."

He spotted the petroglyphs right away. "Hey, look at that! Are they real?"

"I'd risk my professional reputation on it. And there are probably Indian artifacts around the fire pit and charcoal remains proving early use. The drawings are so primitive I'd guess they were several hundred years old."

"That's terrific, sweetheart. Looks like you're going to be famous."

"If I survive."

He did a mental double take. "What do you mean?"

"To properly handle a find like this I should have a staff of ten. Right now I've got a half-dozen volunteers who help out around the museum a few hours a week. They're all like Estelle. Sweet and well-meaning but not experienced in archaeology and not even physically fit enough to handle a job that's likely to entail at least some excavation."

"So hire somebody."

She sighed. "If the museum had an endowment of a couple of million dollars, I'd do just that. Trust me. The current balance in the checkbook is closer to two thousand than to two million."

"It takes that much to run this kind of a show?" That was a lot of cash, even for King. He'd have to liquidate a lot of assets to come up with that much green. Not an easy task.

"And without the proper backing..." Something that looked suspiciously like tears pooled in her eyes. "Darn it all. This is *my* find. I should be able to develop it. Not some big museum from San Francisco or LA that could pressure the park service to get their cooperation. A museum like mine doesn't have squat in the way of influence, much less enough money to handle the job professionally."

"Take it easy, Maggie. You'll find a way." He slipped his hand along the column of her neck. He wished there were something in his life as important as the museum was to Maggie. Inheriting wealth managed to devalue everything else. The only thing he'd ever cared about was Maggie. And the best thing he could do for her was walk away. That was a hell of a lousy choice. "There's still Whitecloud's treasure—"

"You and your darn treasures. It's probably as much of a hoax as that cockamamy story was in New Mexico." In utter frustration she kicked at a rock resting beside the petroglyphs. The stone moved.

She gaped at what the slight movement had revealed. It couldn't be . . . yet Whitecloud's story had involved a cave, Indians and a fortune in gold. Margaret's head spun. Could dreams really come true? All of them?

A leather strap stuck out from beneath the rock. An old leather strap.

Her breath lodged in her throat. "King . . . ?" With knees gone rubbery, she squatted down next to the rock. The treasure. If they'd really found the treasure, the museum, the archaeological dig, everything could be hers. "Give me a hand. Careful, now. We don't want to . . ." Her hands shook.

The rock moved easily. Under it, hidden in a shallow depression, was a leather pouch with U.S. Army stamped on the flap. The pouch wasn't large. More like an oversize wallet. And definitely old.

She frowned. It seemed to Margaret that a fortune in gold ought to come in a bigger package. At the least she would have expected saddlebags stuffed with coins.

Suspicion tugged at her awareness. She tried to suppress the thought that she'd been the victim of a hoax. Again.

"Let me," King said, moving the rock out of the way with considerable confidence. This had to be it—the treasure Whitecloud had told him about. Why else would he have felt the old Indian's presence so strongly?

He caught Maggie's eye and knew she was holding her breath. Truth be known, so was he. He'd like nothing more than to give her treasures untold, the riches of the world. In the end, though, he doubted she'd thank him for the miserable life that went with too much money.

He lifted the pouch and folded back the flap. It sure as hell didn't feel heavy enough for any million dollars' worth of gold.

"Hold out your hands," he ordered.

"King, I can't..."

"Do it, sweetheart. Whatever is here belongs to you. You've definitely earned it."

Slowly he poured the contents into her cupped hands. The solid sound of gold clinking against gold was loud in the depths of the cave. When he was finished, twenty ten-dollar gold pieces rested in her palms.

"This was the whole army payroll?" she asked incredulously. "I came all this way, got shot at, nearly died in an avalanche and then was kidnapped, all for this?" Wild-eyed, she shook her head. "That's not possible! There has to be more."

Setting the coins aside, she started to dig around the rock with her bare hands. Her fingers dug into the hard-packed dirt.

King could understand why she was so frantic. Even given the collector value of the coins, he doubted the sawbucks were worth anywhere near a million dollars. He mentally shook an angry fist at Whitecloud. Maggie deserved far more. "Maybe you can use these coins as seed money."

"Are you kidding?" Her voice rose to a hysterical pitch. "This is nice if you're into gathering souvenirs, but it won't even begin to cover the breakage that idiot Luke did at the museum."

"I'll make it up to you, Maggie."

"Sure you will. Just like you vanished from Santa Fe when you'd promised to help me search for artifacts." Margaret glared at him with all the fury she could muster. The man didn't give a fig about money. The treasure didn't mean diddly-squat to him. Multimillionaires were like that, she supposed. "This is *my* museum we're talking about. A museum that's very likely to go bankrupt unless I come up with a miracle."

He dragged the backs of his fingers gently along her cheek. "I'm sorry, Maggie girl."

Fighting unwelcome tears of frustration, she shrugged off his touch. There wasn't any more gold here, she realized. And yelling at King wasn't going to change that. Digging in the dirt would only get her more broken fingernails.

When she blew out a resigned sigh King grinned at her, that silly, cocky smile that could be so infuriating.

"Guess I blew it again," he said.

"Royally."

"Then let's get out of here." He'd put the coins back in the pouch and now he slipped the leather strap over her shoulder. "While you were exploring the cave, I was taking a look at the map. I think we can ski out of this place and get you back to civilization."

She groaned. He wasn't through with her yet. There'd be another chance for him to do her in. "Ski?"

"Sure. We'll use Smooth-Head and Little John's gear. The fit ought to be close enough. We'll be back to civilization in a couple of days."

Margaret wasn't so sure she ever wanted to return to reality. Not if it meant King would go off on another adventure, leaving her behind. Again. And she knew he would. No wife, no kids. That's what he'd said. Simply one wild-goose chase after another. *What an incredibly wasteful way to live.* And she'd probably destroyed her museum in her effort to keep up with him. "Last night when we crashed, I didn't think you even knew where we were," she pointed out.

"I've done some calculating. Basically, all we have to do is go south until we find the Tuolumne River, then follow it to the Hetch Hetchy dam. Should be a piece of cake. There's a road from there that will take us out of the park."

It all sounded a bit too easy. Particularly where King was concerned. "I'm not exactly an expert skier," she warned. "And your ankle is still bothering you."

"We'll take it slow," he promised.

She glanced back toward the cave entrance. "We can't go anywhere till it quits snowing."

"Spring storms don't usually last very long."

"In that case, why don't I check to see if there's anything in the packs we can eat for breakfast."

King stood aside to let her pass. Getting Maggie safely out of Yosemite was what he wanted, he reminded himself, even as he watched the sexy sway of her hips. She moved with such unconscious grace it made him ache to have her again. But soon...very soon he would have to turn his back on her and walk away. He suspected that getting into a wrestling match with another wolverine would be a whole hell of a lot easier.

BY MIDMORNING THE SKIES had begun to clear.

It took a while for Margaret to get into the rhythmic cadence of poling and sliding across the snow. On level traverses she seemed to be all right. Going uphill wasn't so easy. Downhill was the scariest. Too often she picked up speed and found herself out of control, unable to slow her descent without losing her balance and tumbling head over heels.

As the day wore on, the heavy pack they'd inherited from Smooth-Head Luke felt more and more like an anchor on her back.

Mindlessly she contoured the slopes in King's wake, past rocky cols blown clear of snow and gnarled foxtail pines that leaned permanently in the direction of the wind. Her lungs labored with each step. Time fused into putting one foot in front of the other.

Finally King called a rest stop.

Margaret sank to the ground and shrugged off her pack, placing the army pouch with the gold coins in it on the snow beside her.

"Maybe if we made a fire, someone would see the smoke and come investigate," she suggested.

King handed her a bag of trail mix. "Problem is, it might be Smooth-Head who showed up, not a friendly park ranger on a rescue mission."

"You're paranoid, King. How would Luke be able to come after us? We crashed his helicopter, remember?"

"*One* of his helicopters. He's probably got hangars full of 'em. Plus a personal jet and a yacht or two."

She munched on a handful of raisins and nuts. It was somehow reassuring that a guy like Luke ate the same food as ordinary people. "Aren't any of your fellow treasure hunters just normal folks?" *With mortgages to pay and kids to raise....*

"I don't think so."

Too bad. Because that was what Margaret wanted out of life. Sure, it didn't sound very exciting compared to the way King lived, but it was what she'd dreamed about all her life. That, and being the curator of a well-respected museum. Was it really so much to ask?

"You're a lot like my father," she mused aloud, almost to herself. "Except he never had two extra pennies to pinch together."

"How's that?" King leaned back against the pack he'd propped in the snow.

For a moment she studied the blue of his eyes, the rugged angles of his face, his usually smooth-shaven cheeks now roughened by whiskers, and wished anew that either she or King were a different kind of person. "A dreamer. Two feet planted firmly in midair. In his case, he is a very *un*successful inventor. He's always coming up with some crazy new scheme. My mother used to plead with him to get some sort of an ordinary job. She still does. He tried it a couple of times." She shook her head. "It never works out."

"Not everyone has to work a nine-to-five job."

"Of course not. It's just that . . ." She tugged her lower lip between her teeth and drew in a painful breath. "He gets so involved in his projects. When I was a kid, his would-be inventions always seemed more important than anything I could do. I would have had to practically burn down his garage—he called it his laboratory—in order to get his attention."

"What you do with the museum is important."

"Do you think so?" Not many people thought musty old exhibits were worth their time of day. "Is that why Luke found copies of *The Curator's Quarterly* at your house?"

"Well, ah . . ." He levered himself to his feet. Old Smooth-Head had a big mouth. King hadn't wanted

Maggie to know he'd made a point of following her career. "The magazine keeps me up-to-date on new discoveries. You know, the latest sunken treasures. Inca burial sites. That sort of thing," he lied.

Spearing her fingers through her hair, Margaret realized she should have known better than to go fishing for information. For whatever reasons, King was in the treasure-hunting business. She shouldn't have hoped for something more personal. At least, not on a long-term basis.

She slipped her skis back on and slid the pouch strap over her shoulder. "What will you do when we get out of the mountains?" she asked, a painful lump forming in her throat. Dear God, she was going to have to get over him all over again.

"A while back I heard about some White Russian artifacts that were hidden before the revolution. Jeweled goblets, Fabergé eggs, that sort of thing. Relics left over from friends of the czar, I'm told. Now that the East is more open to tourists, I thought maybe I'd take a look."

She hefted her pack. "Be sure to send me a postcard from Siberia," she grumbled, striding off in front of him. She jammed her poles hard into the snow, shoving off at each step with all of the muscle power she had.

The man was incorrigible. He had no time for her—not in the life he chose to lead. She'd known that all along. There was no reason at this late date for her vision to be blurring and her chin quivering. She'd had her romantic interlude. Twice was enough. No harm done. Now it was time to get back to the business of living in the real world.

"Hey, wait up, Maggie girl." King herringboned after her at a half run, his ankle zinging him with every step. He'd really made her mad this time. Maybe it was better that way. He didn't want her left with any illusions. He was no good for her and knew it.

She angled up a slope, moving faster than she had all morning. One tough lady, King decided. She'd be all right. He wasn't quite so sure about himself. Somehow the years ahead of him seemed more bleak and empty now than those he'd already survived. Not a pleasant thought.

They'd almost reached the summit of a saddle pass between two ridges when he heard the first distinctive sound of helicopter rotors.

He cursed under his breath. Smooth-Head simply wouldn't give up. He'd always been that way. And dangerous. Maggie had been damn lucky to survive being kidnapped by the guy.

"Come on, sweetheart," he shouted, catching up with her. "We've got company. Drop your pack and let's hightail it into the woods."

Margaret looked over her shoulder and saw the helicopter racing toward them, low and evil looking. From King's reaction, she knew it had to be Luke on their tail again.

"We'll give them the gold," she pleaded. "I don't give a damn about the money."

"Don't you remember the potshots they took at the helicopter when we borrowed it? We were just lucky the thing didn't blow up when he hit the gas tank. Smooth-Head doesn't take kindly to people who mess with his property, particularly if he's found out we pranged his bird pretty bad.''

Totaled it was a better description. Didn't the man carry insurance? she wondered, then realized that both Luke and King were definitely in an assigned-risk category. In terms of her heart, so was she.

Following King's lead, she unhooked her pack and let it slip to the ground, then skied after him.

They'd topped the rise, and it was downhill now. They zigzagged their way through the trees, making turns as tightly as they could in the soft snow, Margaret barely able to keep her balance. She ducked and swiveled, trying to avoid pine branches that reached out to snap at her face. The tails of her skis skidded from one side to the other. An Olympic candidate she wasn't. Survival was the best she could hope for.

King was doing better. Far more agile and experienced than she, his knees were springier, his hips rotating easily from side to side.

Darn it all. Would he always lead her on such a merry chase?

As the trees thinned he slowed and looked over his shoulder to check on her progress. She bore down on him fast.

Then she saw it. Just beyond King a great yawning chasm lay in their downward path. Unavoidable. Deadly dangerous.

Her eyes widened in terror and a scream escaped from her throat. ''The river!''

She tried to slow down. No good. She was out of control, slipping and sliding pell-mell toward the edge of the cliff. The sound of fast-moving water roared in her ears.

King reached out to grab her, but missed her windmilling arms. He frantically tried to keep up with her, fear written all over his face. As they went over the precipice together, shooting out into the air as if they'd been launched by a Cape Kennedy rocket, she saw him mouth something. The sound of his words was snatched away by the wind.

"What?" she cried as the boiling ribbon of water below her widened into a raging river fed by snow melt and the spring thaw. She failed to hear his response as she fell like a rock toward the bottom of the canyon.

She plunged into the icy water that was white and frothy and tasted of silt. The current yanked the skis from her feet, tumbling her over and over, and she released her grip on the poles. Like a human pinball she was battered from boulder to boulder, her lungs painfully in need of oxygen.

Her head popped up and she gasped for air, catching a quick glimpse of King before being driven underwater again.

A powerful force snatched at the back of her jacket. She fought against it, kicking and thrashing, trying to reach the surface again. It seemed like an eternity before she realized it was King trying to pull her up out of the water by the collar of her jacket.

He hauled her bruised and scraped body into shallow water, then up onto a sandy bank. Gasping, moving slowly on all fours, she dragged welcome gulp after gulp of air into her lungs, coughing and sputtering. Her hair hung like lanky blond seaweed in front of her face.

Vaguely she was aware that the army pouch with the gold coins was gone, but at the moment it didn't seem to matter. She doubted it ever would.

Before she had entirely caught her breath she looked up at King, who was kneeling next to her. "What did you say?" she asked between gasps. "When we were falling off that cliff, what did you say?"

"I, ah, I don't remember."

"Say it, damn it. I want to hear you say it." She'd get those words pried out of him if it was the very last thing she ever did.

"I said..." He dragged what was obviously a reluctant breath up from his lungs. "I said...I love you."

"That's what I thought." She collapsed onto her back. The weakest of smiles played at the corners of her mouth, and she was filled with a feeling more of relief than of some wondrous accomplishment. "Your timing's lousy, McDermott."

He grinned down at her. "Always has been, sweetheart."

Overhead, a helicopter hovered between the canyon walls. Across its belly the initials C.A.P. were emblazoned in red. The Civil Air Patrol had come to the rescue a little too late. Margaret's heart was already lost beyond redemption, and it wouldn't do her a damn bit of good. King would still leave her. And she'd managed to save very little of herself in the process of losing her heart.

THE ANTISEPTIC SMELL of the hospital mixed with the scent of Margaret's uneaten breakfast, the scrambled eggs growing cold on the plate at her bedside. Gingerly she pulled on a pair of jeans and snapped the waist closed.

"Are you sure you're all right to go home?" her mother asked, handing her a yellow T-shirt stenciled with the logo of an annual Sierra ten-kilometer run.

"I'm fine. Just a few contusions and bruises, the doctor says." Through the window she could see the morning sun glistening off the office buildings of downtown Modesto. Below her room the helicopter landing pad, where the Civil Air Patrol had delivered her and King the previous afternoon, was empty. "Is Dad coming to the hospital?"

"He was going to, but he got a call from one of his prospective backers. You know how he is when he starts talking to someone about his inventions."

A familiar empty sensation twisted in Margaret's chest. "Yes, I know." She tried to swallow her hurt and failed. "How have you stood it all these years, Mother? Married to a man who never has time for his family?"

"Whatever are you talking about? All men are like that. Wrapped up in their own little worlds." Alyse Townsend's hand passed over her graying hair in a futile effort to smooth the bluntly cut strands. The five-and-dime barrette she wore simply drooped at a more awkward angle. "At least I always knew where to find your father."

Out in the garage totally involved in his own project, not giving a fig about Margaret or anyone else.

"The point is, neither your father nor I can understand why on earth you went off with that McDermott fellow at all. To find a treasure? What a ridiculous notion." Alyse fussed about, straightening the bed.

"We found the gold coins." All twenty of them. Hardly a find worth major headlines.

"I don't see anything that looks like gold to me. Seeing's believing, I always say."

Margaret slid her feet into tennis shoes. Along with the bruises, she had acquired a good many aches and pains that made almost any movement painful. At this point she had only two speeds—slow and stop. "I guess I lost the army pouch. The strap probably broke. I got thrown around quite a bit." The gold was no doubt at the bottom of the Tuolumne River. Not that it would have been enough to restore her Indian museum, or finance a significant archaeological dig, but she was sorry about losing what she and King had risked their necks to find.

"I really thought I'd raised you to be more responsible, Margaret, dear. Going off like that... Whatever will that nice Robert Duran and his children think of you?"

"I have no idea, Mother." Nor did she particularly care. Last night had been a haze of X rays, tests and police questioning, all of which was followed by a shot that had knocked her out for more than twelve hours. She wondered if King had received the same treatment. Or if he had already skipped out of the hospital, leaving her to face the morning alone.

"Well, Robert is waiting downstairs for you. It was so nice of him to drive all the way in from the mountains so early in the morning to pick you up. I'm sure he had to make arrangements for someone else to take his classes today. Probably had to pay a substitute out of his own money."

"Robert is a very thoughtful, generous man." She borrowed her mother's comb and dragged it through her hair a few times. Looking in the mirror, she wondered if anyone else would see a different woman than the one who had left Glenville only a few days ago. Probably not.

Her chin quivered and she mentally cursed herself. The man couldn't have gone off and left her again.

Trying for a casual tone, she asked, "Is King still around?"

"I'm sure I wouldn't know. The last I heard, he was still talking to the police."

"Police? They were back again this morning?"

"Well, a woman died, you know. You don't just walk away from a thing like that."

"She tried to kill us."

"I understand," Alyse said in a condescending way. "But really, dear, you simply shouldn't associate with people like that. They say she'd already shot one man. Some sort of an Indian guru in Malibu, for heaven's sake."

Whitecloud. As far as Margaret could tell, King's only real friend. "I'll keep that in mind for the future."

"And then there were those poor park rangers she locked up in some shack at Tuolumne Meadows. It's a wonder they got out of there without a bad case of frostbite, to say the very least. They wouldn't have, either, except for those skiers who got suspicious and called for help on the ranger's radio."

Good for Crazy Arnold and his friends. "How did anyone know where to come looking for us? And that we were in trouble?" She didn't imagine Luke had spread the word.

"An airline pilot flying between Los Angeles and Reno happened to hear your call for help, and the Civil Air Patrol started a search when the weather cleared. They weren't even sure it wasn't some kind of a crank call. You're a very lucky young lady, my dear."

"Yes, I suppose I am." Margaret dropped the comb back into her mother's purse. At the moment she didn't feel very lucky. Not if King had already left. She kept glancing at the door. If he was walking around in one piece, which was evidently the case since he'd been talking to the police, then he should have shown up to see her. Surely he'd be concerned about her.

Anxiety formed a lump in her throat. She was afraid to walk out the door for fear King wouldn't be there, would already be on his way to Siberia in search of White Russian treasure.

"Are you ready, dear? We don't want to keep Robert waiting any longer than we have to. And I have a million errands to run." Her mother clutched her purse to her narrow waist. "It will take us a few minutes to check you out of the hospital. You do have insurance, don't you?"

"Yes, I'm insured." For about half of the bill, she suspected. Lord knew where she'd come up with the rest of the money. Particularly if she found herself in the unemployment lines. She picked up the trapper's diary from the bedside table. At least she could return the book to the museum's archives, although it was somewhat the worse for wear. Fortunately she'd had the small volume tucked in an inside pocket of her jacket, and it had stayed put during her unexpected dunking in the river.

"Well, come along, then." Alyse pulled open the door and walked out into the hallway.

He was standing there, his thumbs tucked into his jeans, his hands framing his lean hips, his usual cocky grin on his face. Somehow the small Band-Aid on his cheek only managed to emphasize his virility, as though he could go through all of the perils they'd experienced with only a mere cut that was no more than he might have gotten from shaving.

Her heart nearly burst in her chest she was so glad to see King. He hadn't left her alone.

"Hi, there, Maggie girl. You're lookin' good." His silver-blue eyes surveyed her in a quick, licentious inventory, noting her tight-fitting jeans and the old T-shirt her mother had brought from home. "Thought

I'd stick around long enough to say goodbye. I've got a flight scheduled out of LA...."

Margaret didn't hear the rest. She felt light-headed, with white noise rushing through her head. A pulse pounded at her temple. He'd only come to say goodbye. Somehow she should have known.

He fell into step beside her as she walked toward the elevators. He kept talking, but all she could hear were his damn snakeskin boots clicking with each of his long-legged strides on the floor. He was going to leave her. She'd forced him to make an admission of words that simply weren't true. He had other challenges to face, ones that didn't include room for her.

So much like her father.

Alyse Townsend stepped into the elevator first, followed by Margaret and King.

Facing the door, Margaret watched the elevator lights call out the floors with excruciating precision— three, two, one. In a moment King would be gone. The pain in her chest was so intense she could barely draw a breath.

The doors opened onto the lobby.

She felt the warm, caressing heat of King's hand at her elbow. In the next instant she was blinded by flashbulbs popping. As she stepped out of the elevator a dozen or more people surrounded her, shoving and pushing up against her, most of them sticking a microphone in her face. She felt a moment of terror, of total disorientation. Instantly she lost track of her mother, aware only of the surging press of people and King beside her.

"Ms. Townsend. What's your relationship with Mr. McDermott?" one man asked.

She swiveled her head in the questioner's direction. "Relationship?"

"Does Mr. McDermott's wealth intimidate you, Ms. Townsend?" a dark-haired woman inquired, licking the point of her pencil and lowering it to a notepad she carried.

"How do you feel having your name linked with the most eligible bachelor—"

"I don't think—"

"Thank you, ladies, gentlemen," King forcefully inserted. "We have no comment at this time."

Another flashbulb went off in her face. Margaret let out a startled gasp.

"What did you do up in those mountains?" another reporter persisted, a nasty insinuation in his voice.

"Was your kidnapping, Ms. Townsend, related to the famous case of—"

"Was there a ransom—"

King angled her off to the side of the lobby where she couldn't hear the rest of the questions. She felt as if she'd been assaulted. Her legs were weak.

"What on earth is going on?" she asked as King shoved open an emergency door.

Suddenly they were out on a sidewalk, the bright Modesto sun making her blink. Robert Duran stood beside the open door of his Chevy van. Tall and lanky with thinning hair, he had the healthy good looks of a marathon runner. His gray eyes were filled with kindness.

Her heart beating way too fast, she glanced at King. His sensuous lips were drawn into a grim line.

"You see how it is, Maggie girl. I'm nothing more than fodder to them. A few lines of copy. A twenty-second sound bite on tonight's TV news. And whatever they do, it will bring out the loonies with more threats. I couldn't put anyone through that. Certainly not someone I love."

He handed her off to Robert then, like an unwelcome baton in some macabre relay race, she thought, fighting down a wave of hysteria. He couldn't tell her goodbye. Not if he loved her.

But a moment later Robert's van had taken her out of the hospital parking lot. Prepared to jump out of the moving vehicle and run back the way they had come, she glanced over her shoulder.

King was already gone.

Chapter Thirteen

Fog lay heavily over the Southern California coast, thick and gray and depressing, smelling of salt and decaying seaweed the tide had dragged onto the beach.

With his fingertips tucked into the hip pockets of his jeans, King stared out to sea. Not that there was much to see.

He curled his bare toes into the cold, gritty sand.

Two weeks since he'd seen Maggie; fourteen days since he'd run the backs of his fingers across her smooth cheek, an eternity since he'd held her in his arms.

"Damn," he muttered under his breath.

The thought of going to the old Soviet Union held no appeal. Forget the rumors of incredible treasures that had circulated among his associates. Traveling to the far reaches of Siberia, or anywhere else for that matter, simply didn't seem worth the effort. The spark he'd had for life had faded; his purpose—such as it had been—had vanished in the mist.

With weary resignation King looked out to sea again.

From out of the fog came the distinctive rattle of Indian beads. King groaned.

"Not now, Whitecloud. I don't feel like dealing with—"

"I've been waiting for you in Siberia. What's taking you so long?" The image of the old Indian's face floated in the fog, rising and falling with the gentle lap of the waves.

"I changed my mind."

"Others have heard the rumors of great wealth. They will soon be coming. If you do not hurry, we will lose the treasure to them."

King had already lost the only treasure that mattered. Lost it not once, but twice. *Maggie.* "I'm not interested."

An unexpected wave, larger than the others, rolled up onto the beach. It drove King back up the sand a few steps but not before getting his jeans wet to his knees. He hated the feeling of clinging denim.

"I grow impatient with you, my young friend."

"Swell. Then go haunt somebody else." King couldn't concentrate on anything except the fact that he had handed Maggie over to that schoolteacher. The guy was about as square as they come. Solid. A family man. Boring. He'd talked to the man, for heaven's sake—when they were arranging for Duran to slip Maggie away from the press at the hospital. He'd known the guy cared for Maggie. Not just a little, but a whole damn lot.

That hurt King. Like hell. Right in the middle of his gut. Like a miserable combination of Montezuma's revenge and a samurai sword.

The thought of Robert Duran messing around with *his* Maggie was driving him crazy and had been for the past two weeks.

A wave twice as big as any other raced out of the fog, slammed into King and toppled him backward onto his butt. "Hey, cut that out!" he objected.

The foggy image shifted across the water in an angry swirl. "Do you plan to do nothing more than walk on the beach the rest of your life?"

"Hell, no!" Now King was really getting mad. Nobody, not Whitecloud or Duran, was going to push him around. Feeling a surge of adrenaline, he scrambled back to his feet and shook his fist at the swirling fog. "I'm going after Maggie, drag her into my arms and kiss her senseless. That's what I'm going to do. I'll show 'em no stodgy schoolteacher can mess with *my* woman." He'd shouted the words before King had fully realized that was exactly what he wanted to do. Intended to do. Right now.

The image snorted a mocking laugh. "And then you'll leave her again."

"No, not this time. I'm done treasure hunting. *Fini.*" If Maggie wanted boring and stodgy, then that was what Maggie would get. With him.

"Ah. I see. Suddenly all those would-be kidnappers mean nothing? They will come after you, you know. You have always said so."

So he had. But was it true?

Sure, he still got an occasional threat. But that was because his name was on the masthead of a major newspaper. That title brought with it a whole slew of unwelcome notoriety. Added to his multimillionaire status, and a very visible estate on Lake Michigan, he was a target for a lot of crazies.

But maybe, just maybe, there was a way out of his dilemma. One he'd never before considered. Perhaps it was the fears of his parents that had blinded him to other alternatives.

With new resolve he turned his back on the fog and marched up the beach to the house. There was a lot of work to be done. This was no time to stand around talking to some old ghost. Not when Maggie might already be in Duran's clutches.

Behind him he heard the sighing sound of Indian beads drifting out on the current and the quiet lap of waves along the beach. He glanced over his shoulder to discover the image of Whitecloud was gone.

King smiled. Deep in his gut he suspected that someday, when he least expected it, Whitecloud would reappear.

"YOU SEEMED EXTRA QUIET tonight, Margaret. Is there something wrong?" Robert Duran, his forearms circled with soapsuds, handed her a plate to dry.

"I'm sorry. Guess I'm just tired."

"The girls have missed you lately. I think they enjoyed making dinner for you."

"They're both adorable. You're a very lucky man." She placed the dried plate onto a stack of similar dishes in the cupboard of the small kitchen. Robert's house was a modest one with a brick walkway from the street to the front porch and a backyard shaded by pines. The living room and dining room formed a standard L shape, and the kitchen wasn't the sort that would ever be featured in *House Beautiful.* It might not seem like much to aspire to, living in a home like this and raising a family here, but that's what Margaret had always wanted. Until King had dragged her off to Yosemite. And she didn't dare think about that. "The girls might want to practice their cake-making technique just a little bit more," she suggested as lightly as she could, ignoring the sudden lump the thought of King had brought to her throat.

"It was pretty lopsided, I admit." He handed her another plate, his gentle smile filled with understanding. "The last couple of years I've been hoping I'd find somebody who could teach the girls all the things their mother would have if she'd lived long enough."

Her gaze slid away from his gray eyes. "You're doing a fine job with them."

"I like to think so, but it isn't always easy. They can be a handful."

At ages six and eight, Rebecca and Susie were easy-to-love angels and little minxes rolled into two lovely, fair-haired packages. Margaret could see a lot of Robert in his two children and was struck, almost like a physical blow, with the thought that she'd like to hold a child who resembled King as closely—a child she'd never have a chance to bear. With heart-wrenching desperation she wanted to see King's silver-blue eyes looking up at her from the face of his daughter, or that cocky grin of his tilting the lips of his son. If she only had some part of him to love, to hold on to—

The soapy plate slipped from her hands and she drew a sobbing breath as it shattered on the linoleum floor.

"Oh, Robert, I'm so sorry." A tear she couldn't quite prevent escaped to edge down her cheek.

"Hey, it's all right. It's just an old plate." He took the drying cloth from her hands and gently restrained her from dropping to her knees to sweep up the mess.

"I'm not usually so...careless." Her breath hitched. She had hoped after surviving a couple of weeks without King she would have gotten over this terrible tendency to burst into tears at the least little provocation.

"You've probably been working too hard."

"The museum was a mess," she agreed, nodding and pursing her lips so her chin wouldn't wobble. "I've been trying to restore what I could after all the vandalism." Smooth-Head Luke and his soprano buddy were definitely on her all-time enemies list. They were also among the missing, and probably out of the country, as far as the police could determine. "And I've been sending grant requests to every foundation I could think of. There's so much that needs to be done for the museum."

He gently cupped and lifted her chin. "Based on those dark smudges I've noticed under your eyes the last few weeks, you're not sleeping enough, either."

Trying for an offhand shrug, she dryly said, "Thanks for the compliment."

"I've never billed myself as a mind reader, but my guess is those dark circles under your eyes and your bursting into tears because you dropped an already chipped plate has something to do with Kingsley McDermott."

She twisted her head away from Robert's hand because she couldn't lie to his face. He'd very likely see the truth in her eyes. "Don't be silly. McDermott doesn't mean a thing to me."

"Funny. The day he and I met, I got the distinct impression *you* meant a whole lot to him."

"Well, you got it wrong, Robert." Whirling away, she headed for the living room to pick up her sweater. King didn't want her. He'd made that abundantly clear. "I've really got to go. Tell the girls—"

With his long legs Robert was quicker and more agile than Margaret. He blocked her path at the door, folding his arms across his chest.

"Look, Margaret, I'm very fond of you, and so are my children. I'd hoped we might be right for each other. But I've known for a long time the spark or whatever you call it between a man and woman just isn't there for us. I do think we're friends, though, and I suspect you need a friend more than anything else right now."

"You're making a mountain out of a—"

"You love him, don't you?" he persisted.

She swallowed hard. "I don't want to." Robert was the kind of man she wanted to love. Solid. Dependable. Down-to-earth. And he'd just rejected her. So much for today's ego-building experience.

"Why don't you want to love him? He seemed like a nice-enough guy."

"He's an adventurer!" she blurted out in an angry shout. "Every time I'm anywhere near the man it's like I'm caught in the middle of a remake of *Raiders of the Lost Ark*. He's an absolute lunatic. He lives in some kind of a dream world where everything is possible. It's crazy! I can't handle that. I want dinner at six and slippers in front of the fireplace. Peace and quiet. Not some wild, insane scheme taking me to the ends of the earth."

When Margaret paused for a split second Robert said, "He makes you feel alive."

She stared at him, surprised by his insight. Softly she replied, "It's like I'm a black-and-white photo, and then King comes into my life, turning everything into Technicolor. The reds are redder, the blues more intense. I can't seem to catch my breath. I don't know how to explain it." Studying Robert, such a straight-arrow guy, she wondered if he had ever experienced the same sensations. "Was it the same with you and your wife?" she asked, hoping she wasn't prying too much.

A wistful look came into his eyes. "Maybe the colors were a little more muted than you're describing, but, yeah, we were pretty darn good together."

She blew out a sigh. "I'm sorry I can't be the right one for you, Robert. You're a very special man."

With an obvious effort he brought himself back from his own memories. "So why don't you get on your pony and go find McDermott? Tell him how you feel."

"He's not into commitments. Marriage is not his cup of tea."

"That's what every man says—" Robert's lips curled into a smile "—until some woman teaches him different."

"He has his reasons. They're good ones."

"No more than excuses, would be my bet."

She looked at him skeptically. "You think so?"

"You can count on it, friend." He looped his arm around her shoulders and gave her a hug. "Go join him at whatever adventure he has in mind and he'll come around faster than you might think."

"I can't do that. I have responsibilities. What about the museum?"

"What about it?" he asked quietly, raising his eyebrows in question.

AFTER A SHAKY GOODBYE to Robert, Margaret drove home to her own apartment and a sleepless night. Not that the lack of sleep was anything new to her in the past few weeks. But now she'd added to her troubles with a conscience that was on a rampage, warring with her heart.

Her museum, her career, all that she cared about were on the line. She didn't want to give any of that up. Even so, sometime past dawn she picked up her phone. Years ago in Santa Fe, King had given her a

Malibu number. In a weak moment she'd actually called him, only to get an answering machine that informed her he wasn't home and wasn't expected for some time. She hadn't had the nerve to leave a message. It wouldn't have mattered, she realized with an awful sense of futility. He'd known where to find her.

All this time she'd kept his number on a little scrap of paper tucked into a cubbyhole at the back of her rolltop desk. More than once she'd been struck by how absurdly sentimental her actions had been. But she'd never quite gotten up the courage to throw that small piece of paper away.

With shaking hands she dialed the number now. It rang three times before she heard the click of a response. Heart aching, she held her breath.

"Hey, this is McDermott," the recorded voice said. "If you're trying to reach me, forget it. I'm off on the most exciting adventure of my life. With any luck at all, I won't be at this number again."

Margaret held the phone in her hand, her fingers aching with the effort, until there was nothing left but a dial tone, followed by a mechanical female voice suggesting if she needed assistance, she should call 911.

She didn't think that would help.

Slowly Margaret hung up. She was too late. The call of White Russian treasure had lured King away. She could hardly blame him. If her father had had a chance, he probably would have gone off to some faraway land to pursue his inventions without the bothersome presence of his family.

She blinked and swallowed past the lump in her throat. The museum was what mattered. The best damn little museum in the country. She'd see to that... and hated that she couldn't seem to stop her chin from quivering.

MARGARET PUNCHED the back-space bar on the ancient manual typewriter. Someday the museum would have not just a self-correcting electric typewriter, she promised herself, but a full-fledged computer with state-of-the-art word processing—if she could ever talk some foundation into giving her a reasonable grant. So far she hadn't come close to getting a dime out of anyone. The poor board of directors had been forced to plan a whole series of garage sales and pancake breakfasts in the faint hope of keeping the museum afloat.

My fault, she kept thinking with considerable guilt. As for the petroglyphs, a San Francisco museum was actively pursuing funding sources in competition with her to develop the project.

With a sigh she carefully slid the square of correction paper in place and struck the wrong key again. The Miwok Indians must have had better equipment to work with than she did, she grumbled.

The bell on the museum's front door tinkled its welcome to visitors. She jumped at the sound. Lately she'd been a nervous wreck, even being abrupt with her well-intentioned volunteers when she should be thanking her lucky stars they were willing to help her out all they could.

She glanced over her shoulder to see the mail carrier coming toward her.

"Hi, Sharon, you're early today." Margaret wondered how many more foundation turndowns she would get in today's mail, then quickly set the negative thought aside. No sense asking for trouble.

"I've got a special delivery for you. Have to get those out by ten or the supervisor has a fit." The matronly woman walked past the counter with a quick stride and handed Margaret a single envelope. "I need your signature." She supplied a ballpoint pen from her breast pocket.

"Sure." Puzzled, Margaret signed, then noted the return address. She recognized the name as an obscure charitable foundation in the Midwest that gave very small grants to equally enigmatic causes. She hadn't even bothered to ask them for money. If you didn't have a connection with that kind of an outfit, you didn't stand a chance.

Sharon tore the return receipt from the envelope and handed the letter back to Margaret. "Have a good day," she said in a cheerful, businesslike manner, striding toward the door.

Distractedly Margaret called after her, "You, too."

Her curiosity piqued, she opened the envelope and unfolded a two-page letter. A check was paper-clipped to the first page.

Not just an ordinary check, she realized, staring in amazement at the enclosure. It had so many zeros she had to count them twice to make sure she'd done it right the first time. For good measure, she tried it again.

Her knees felt suddenly weak. A wave of light-headedness made her feel dizzy and she reached for the counter to steady herself.

The check, the glorious check with all those beautiful zeros preceded by a numeral five, was made out to Sierra Indian Museum. Enough money to hire a regular staff for a year *plus* begin a thorough archaeological investigation of all of Yosemite.

It had to be some kind of bizarre mistake, she told herself. Or possibly a prank in very poor taste. She had a file folder filled with rejection letters from foundations all across the country. Now, out of the blue...

Her eyes narrowed on the date. Today. *The first of April.*

She almost screamed. What utter cruelty. To try to make an April fool's joke of her efforts to save a floundering museum. To give her one moment of hope only to shatter it again. If she ever found out who'd done this, she'd shove the damn check down his throat! Paper clip and all!

At the sound of the tinkling bell she looked up, forcing some semblance of a smile to her lips.

''Hello, Maggie girl,'' he greeted her in a raspy, familiar voice filled with intimacy.

She saw red. Unbridled, unreasonable fury whipped through her. King had palmed her off on Robert Duran, leaving her brokenhearted, and now he had the unmitigated gall to play an underhanded trick like this.

"You did this, didn't you?" she accused, shaking the letter at him.

His cocky grin and sauntering, booted stride nearly undid her. "Hope it's enough to get you started," he said.

"How could you be so cruel?" Her voice caught on an angry sob. "How could you make fun of me like this? An April fool's prank! I thought you cared!" She picked up the nearest thing on the counter, a small stone mortar, and hurled it at him.

King ducked out of the way. "Hey, Maggie, what's going on? I thought you'd be glad to see me."

"Why don't you leave me alone?" She snatched up the matching pestle. "You're supposed to be in Siberia by now!"

King decided enough was enough. He had no idea what had gone wrong but he wasn't about to stand there playing dodgeball when Maggie was playing hardball with a bunch of miniature boulders.

"Remember the exhibits," he warned, leaping agilely over the counter and taking the stone away from her before she could throw it at him. Then he hauled her into his arms.

She pummeled him with her fists. "You're heartless! Sadistic! Why do you have to torture me—"

He brought his lips down hard on hers. She tasted of sweet fury and he didn't know why. He only knew her flavor was all he'd ever need.

She struggled against him. Relentlessly he fought back in the only way he knew, his tongue darting across her lips, feinting left and right, until she drew a jagged breath that parted her lips. Then he went on a tender attack. Hot. Moist. Insistent.

Within moments Margaret felt herself weakening. Dear God, she'd missed King...and hated him for taunting her now with his cruel joke, and taunting her in her dreams with the memory of his passionate love. He had no right to make her feel this way—so needy and achy she lacked the will to resist.

Tears of defeat burned at the back of her eyes. "Oh, King..." His name escaped her lips in a painful sigh.

King held her tightly, cherishing her, enjoying the feel of supple body pressed along the length of his, murmuring soothing words against her mouth. No question. Maggie was worth a fortune beyond compare. The greatest treasure he would ever hold.

"It's all right, Maggie girl," he said, the pleasurable constriction in his throat making him sound hoarse. He framed her beautiful face between his palms. With his thumb he wiped a tear from her cheek. "Now tell me what's wrong."

"I—I thought you went to Russia." She hiccuped.

"I changed my mind."

"I called you and your message said—" her breath hitched again "—that you weren't ever coming home."

He raised a curious eyebrow. Maggie had called him? That was a surprise.

"And then this stupid check came." She showed him the letter she'd wadded up in her fist. "No foundation is going to send us five times as much as our annual budget in a single check. It's just a moronic practical joke.''

"It's no joke, sweetheart."

"I know this foundation, King," she insisted. "They're listed in the grantsmanship guide. Everybody in the nonprofit business memorizes that book. They never give any money to museums, or Indian research, or anything like that. I didn't even bother to send them an inquiry, much less a full proposal."

"There's been a change of policy."

She frowned. "What do you know about the R.A.M. Foundation?"

He smoothed away the furrows on her forehead with his lips. "If I told you R.A.M. stood for Richard Alexander McDermott III, would that give you a clue? Originally my father set it up in memory of my brother. Now I'm the primary donor."

"You're kidding."

Grinning, he watched her eyes widen in astonishment and then realization dawn. "The Sierra Indian Museum will be getting a check that big, or bigger if you'd like, for as long as you want."

"How is that possible? I didn't think R.A.M. was very well endowed. I mean, nobody can just keep sending out huge checks every year. They'll run out of money."

"Not for a very long time. I've sold off the family newspaper and liquidated everything else that gave me any visibility, including the family homestead—and I didn't leave a forwarding address for the crazies. Then I turned over most of the proceeds to the foundation." He'd been driving his stockbrokers, Realtors and business agents crazy, and loving every minute. "Of course, since I was in a hurry, I had to take about ten cents on the dollar."

Margaret's head spun with the news. "You mean, you gave everything away and now you're broke?"

"Down to my last few million." He shrugged as if he were talking about pocket change. "There're lots of millionaires around. Most of 'em never make the news, whatever their names are. I've lived all of my life trying to make up for the fact that Richie died too soon. I finally realized I don't owe him anything and it's time to stop running scared. My dues are paid in full. From now on nobody will care where I go or what I do." He lowered his voice and brushed a sweet kiss across her lips. "Or that I'm in love with a wonderful woman who I intend to marry as soon as possible."

Her heart leaped into her throat. "You do?"

Digging into his pants pocket, he pulled out a small velvet-covered box. Inside was a narrow gold band that looked to be very old. "I thought this might mean more to you than the diamonds and emeralds I fully intend to buy you. My great-great-grandfather gave his wife this ring. He was a shoemaker who didn't have two extra shillings to pinch together. The ring probably cost him an entire year's wages but, according to family legend, he claimed the woman he loved was worth it. In my case, I quite agree."

"Oh, King . . ." She sighed as he placed the jeweler's box in her hand. "That's the most romantic story."

"Yeah, well, my problem is convincing you to marry a guy who is basically an unemployed bum."

"A guy with a few million dollars in his bank account? Oh, I think I can handle that." Lord, she'd have loved King if the only things he owned were the clothes on his back. And she'd always treasure the ring, a symbol of all he was willing to give. "But eventually you'll have to find something to occupy your time. Like a job?"

"I will?" He looked perplexed.

"Of course. You'd get bored sitting around the house all the time." In King's case, idle hands would surely attract trouble with a capital *T.*

"I've never had a real job," he pointed out, the corners of his eyes crinkling with amusement. "Just who do you think is going to hire me?"

"The Sierra Indian Museum, of course." Margaret was feeling smug and lighthearted and so in love she thought she might burst with joy. "I won't possibly have time to manage the expansion of the museum the grant money will allow, plus supervise new archaeological sites. I'll definitely need an assistant."

"You're going to be my boss?" He arched an eyebrow in a way that brought a warm flutter to her midsection.

She slid her arms up around his neck. "I trust you don't object to working for a woman."

"It may depend on what fringe benefits you're proposing."

"Hmm, let me think." She tangled her fingers in his hair. The wavy strands ensnared her and Margaret knew she'd never stop wanting to touch King in a thousand different ways. "I could promise to sexually harass you every day," she offered suggestively, shifting herself into the nest of his jean-clad hips. Surely the women's movement would forgive her that one little transgression.

"That would be tempting."

"And make you work very long hours. Particularly nights and weekends."

"It's sounding better and better. But won't it be a little awkward—I mean, my working for you and having to address you formally as Mrs. McDermott?"

"I think in your case—" she stood on tiptoe and nipped him lightly on the ear "—you can call me *Maggie*."

"Hmm. Sounds like we're close to an agreement, Maggie, but I do have another question or two."

"Question?" At the moment she'd be much happier with a whole lot of action. She'd be more than willing to forget the museum for the next half hour or so. Damn professional ethics.

"I'd like to know why you called me."

"Oh, that." She shrugged. "It doesn't matter now."

"I think it does."

"Well...I was considering expanding the museum's exhibits," she bluffed. "Sort of a cross-cultural, *glasnost* idea. Anyway, I was thinking about doing a little research on native populations in the old Soviet Union and thought maybe if you were still planning a trip to Siberia..."

King tipped his head back and filled the musty museum with warm laughter. "Oh, sweetheart, you're wonderful!"

A blush heated her cheeks.

Lifting her off her feet so they were face-to-face, he said, "Tell you what, Maggie girl. You'll have that trip to Russia. We'll call it a honeymoon. And while we're there we'll take a little side trip to where I've heard they buried—"

"No, King, we don't need to do that." Lord, what kind of a mess was he going to get her into this time?

"Trust me, Maggie girl. It'll be great."

In spite of herself Margaret laughed. It took only a few quick mental calculations to know that with the hefty check she had in hand, the museum's future would be secure. She'd be free at least some of the time to travel wherever King wanted to go, so he'd never again be out of her sight.

"You're crazy, McDermott, and I love you. I'll go to the ends of the earth with you, if that's what you want. All I ask is that you love me back."

He lowered her into his arms again and held her in a protective embrace. His voice was low and raspy, filled with love. "That's a promise I'll never break."

"Then tell me, King. When I called, your phone message said you were off on some grand new adventure. What were you talking about?"

"Marriage, sweetheart." He gave a quick wink. "The most challenging adventure of all."

Epilogue

Three years later

Maggie curled herself into King's arms as they sat next to each other on the couch. She groaned, shifting her legs beneath her to find a more comfortable position. Her entire body ached.

As she let her gaze slide around the room, she decided their small house in the foothills of the Sierras would never be considered by *House Beautiful* as spacious, but it might earn some points for having the most unusual decorations. One wall boasted an array of African tribal war masks, acquired at frightening personal risk, and another wall held photos of diamonds once owned by the last Russian czar. She and King had barely survived that adventure. She was grateful that the actual diamonds were now safely displayed in a well-secured museum.

The artifacts they'd uncovered in the Sierras were on exhibit at her museum, which was fair, since the R.A.M. Foundation had underwritten the costs of the exploration. She vowed to get back to work as soon as possible.

In the meantime it felt really good to rest her head on her husband's broad shoulder.

"Honey, did you hear something?" he asked.

"Like what?" If it wasn't a crisis, she didn't want to know about it.

"Like a baby laughing."

"King, that's ridiculous. Three-day old babies don't laugh."

"A giggle, then."

"Burps, bubbles and assorted other unpleasant noises. But not giggles."

King moved away from her. "But maybe our little princess is particularly advanced. Don't you think we ought to check?"

"You're going to spoil her," Maggie warned, smiling in spite of herself. Once they had decided it was time to start a family, King had been as eager as she.

"Yeah. Probably." He grinned and Maggie felt warm clear down to her toes, and totally loved, just as she knew their child would be for all of her life. "Let's take a look," he pleaded.

If she'd been to Siberia and Africa with him, and Lord knew where else she'd have to travel in the future, the least she could do was join him on a short safari to their daughter's bedroom. Awkwardly Maggie levered herself to her feet. Arm in arm, they walked down a short hallway. The smell of baby powder and freshly painted walls hovered in the air.

In the bedroom they proudly gazed down at Rachel Renae McDermott, the child they had created together. She looked back at them with silver-blue eyes and a grin that had to be more devilish than simply a case of bothersome gas.

"King, I think we've got a problem."

"You're probably right." From the pristine white bassinet he retrieved a strand of Indian beads that had been draped across the top. "I'm afraid Whitecloud has given up on treasure hunting and found a new calling—as a nanny."

Sighing, Maggie closed her eyes. More trouble was on the way.

Take 4 bestselling love stories FREE

Plus get a FREE surprise gift!

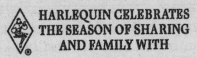

HARLEQUIN CELEBRATES
THE SEASON OF SHARING
AND FAMILY WITH

Friends, Families,
Lovers

Harlequin introduces the latest member in its family of
seasonal collections. Following in the footsteps of the popular
My Valentine, Just Married and *Harlequin Historical Christmas
Stories,* we are proud to present FRIENDS, FAMILIES,
LOVERS. A collection of three new contemporary romance
stories about America at its best, about welcoming others into
the circle of love.... Stories to warm your heart...

By three leading romance authors:

KATHLEEN EAGLE
SANDRA KITT
RUTH JEAN DALE

Available in October, wherever
Harlequin books are sold.

1993 Keepsake

CHRISTMAS

Stories

Capture the spirit and romance of Christmas with KEEPSAKE CHRISTMAS STORIES, a collection of three stories by favorite historical authors. The perfect Christmas gift!

Don't miss these heartwarming stories, available in November wherever Harlequin books are sold:

ONCE UPON A CHRISTMAS by Curtiss Ann Matlock
A FAIRYTALE SEASON by Marianne Willman
TIDINGS OF JOY by Victoria Pade

ADD A TOUCH OF ROMANCE TO YOUR HOLIDAY SEASON WITH KEEPSAKE CHRISTMAS STORIES!

HX93

Fifty red-blooded, white-hot, true-blue hunks from every
State in the Union!

Beginning in May, look for MEN MADE IN AMERICA!
Written by some of our most popular authors, these
stories feature fifty of the strongest, sexiest men, each
from a different state in the union!

Two titles available every other month at your favorite
retail outlet.

In September, look for:

DECEPTIONS by Annette Broadrick (California)
STORMWALKER by Dallas Schulze (Colorado)

In November, look for:

STRAIGHT FROM THE HEART by Barbara Delinsky
(Connecticut)
AUTHOR'S CHOICE by Elizabeth August (Delaware)

You won't be able to resist MEN MADE IN AMERICA!

AMERICAN ROMANCE INVITES YOU TO CELEBRATE A DECADE OF SUCCESS....

It's a year of celebration for American Romance, as we commemorate a milestone achievement—ten years of bringing you the kinds of romance novels you want to read, by the authors you've come to love.

And to help celebrate, Harlequin American Romance has a gift for you! A limited hardcover collection of two of Harlequin American Romance's most popular earlier titles, written by two of your favorite authors:

ANNE STUART—*Partners in Crime*
BARBARA BRETTON—*Playing for Time*

This unique collection will not be available in retail stores and is only available through this exclusive offer.